What people have said about the BUM trilogy (honestly, every word of it is true):

'This book will be in the No. 2 slot by next week' *Sunday Business*

'This book stinks' *Daily Teleguff*

'Ten out of ten readers said their pants preferred it' a talking cat from Doggenham

'Fart? I nearly pooped!' Jeremy Peedle

'A book that registers over 5.5 on the Rectum Scale should be banned as unsuitable for children. This book registers 7.8' Giles Winterbottom, Wee-in-Sea

'Perfect reading for anyone with a loose end' John Bogg, Windchester

ANDY GRIFFITHS

BUMAGEDDON

...THE FINAL PONGFLICT

MACMILLAN CHILDREN'S BOOKS

Teacher's notes for *Bumageddon: The Final Pongflict* are available at
www.panmacmillan.com.au

First published 2005 by Pan Macmillan Australia Pty Limited

First published in the UK 2006 by Macmillan Children's Books
a division of Macmillan Publishers Limited
20 New Wharf Road, London N1 9RR
Basingstoke and Oxford
www.panmacmillan.com

Associated companies throughout the world

ISBN-13: 978-0-330-43370-9
ISBN-10: 0-330-43370-9

3 5 7 9 8 6 4 2

A CIP catalogue record for this book is available from
the British Library.

Typeset by Intype Libra Ltd
Printed and bound in Great Britain by Mackays of Chatham plc, Kent

Dedicated to everybody who has –
or has ever had – a bum

CONTENTS

PROLOGUE

A nd enormous bums will conquer the world and complete and utter devarsetation will follow. Giant brown blobs will rain down upon the Earth for forty days and forty nights. An evil stench will cover the land. And bums will rule the world again as they did in their glorious prehistoric past.

from *The Book of Bumageddon*, Chapter 3006, Verse 258, the Sir Roger Francis Rectum edition.

CHAPTER 1

BLOB

Z ack Freeman looked up and realised that he was about to be squashed by a giant brown blob.

Oh no! he thought. Not a giant brown . . .

But that was all he had time to think before the giant brown blob crashed down on top of him – and everybody else – gathered at the Bum-fighting Academy.

Zack, his bum, his parents, Eleanor Sterne, Silas Sterne, the Kicker, the Smacker and fifty of the best and brightest bum-fighting recruits in the world.

All squashed.

All buried.

All completely giant-brown-blobbified.

CHAPTER 2

BLOBBIFIED

It was a sad end to what had been the proudest and happiest morning of Zack Freeman's life.

Not only had Zack just arrived back on Earth after saving the world from a zombie bum invasion and rescuing his parents from Uranus, but he had also graduated from Silas Sterne's Bum-fighting Academy. In one hand he proudly held his basic bum-fighter's certificate, and in the other a special medal of excellence for his work in the bum-fighting simulator.

Unfortunately, however, none of the challenges Zack had faced so far – either real or simulated – had prepared him for giant-brown-blobbification.

He was way out of his depth.

And sinking fast.

He shut his eyes.

He pinched his nose.

He held his breath.

And then he did . . . well . . . *nothing*.

There was nothing he *could* do.

He could hardly move.

The blob was too thick. And too dark . . . or rather, too brown. Pitch-brown.

He didn't know which way was up.

He didn't know which way was down.

North or south.

East or west.

Zack's mind was racing.

He didn't want to die.

Not yet, anyway.

And especially not inside a giant brown blob.

What if the giant brown blob set hard and became a fossil?

And what if he became a fossil inside the giant brown blob?

And what if one day in the future they dug it up, cracked it open and found him?

He didn't want his body to be put in a glass case and displayed in a museum for schoolchildren to laugh at. 'Eeerggghhh, yuck!' they'd say. 'Blob-boy! Look at the disgusting blob-boy!'

Then again, perhaps that was better than *not* being found and having to spend eternity trapped inside a giant brown blob . . .

Zack shuddered at the thought. With a mighty effort he brought his mind back to the present. He had to stop worrying about what *might* happen in the future and start focusing on what was happening to him *right now*.

And fast.

Zack smiled ruefully as he realised he was still clutching his bum-fighter's certificate. He'd been so proud to receive it, but in this situation a bum-fighter's certificate wasn't even worth the paper it was printed on.

Or was it?

Paper.

The word triggered something inside him – but what? What use was paper?

Suddenly an image of his grandfather flashed into Zack's mind. Percy Freeman – one of the world's first bum-fighters: the Wiper. Armed with only a few rolls of toilet paper and an enormous load of courage, he had wiped some of the deadliest bums on the planet.

Paper.

Wiper.

Even as Zack's oxygen-starved brain was shutting down, the two words forged a fragile, but life-saving, bond in his mind.

Zack knew what he had to do.

He brought the piece of paper up in front of his face.

And started wiping.

CHAPTER 3

WIPE!

Zack wiped.
   He wiped hard.
He wiped fast.
He wiped harder and faster than he'd ever wiped before.
He wiped out a clear space around his head, opened his mouth and took a deep breath. OK, it was bad air, but it was a lot better than *no* air.
Feeling stronger and more hopeful, Zack gripped the certificate with both hands and began the powerful scoop-wipe that he'd learned at the Academy. At the same time he began to kick his feet. It was hard work, but it allowed him to begin tunnelling slowly through the blob.
He still didn't know where he was going, but at least he was going somewhere.
He'd been tunnelling for only a few minutes when he felt a small soft shape moving in front of him.
Although he couldn't see anything in the pitch-brown,

Zack could feel that the shape was in fact a small hand.

Zack recognised it immediately. He reached forward and pulled the hand – and its owner – into his tunnel.

'There you are!' said Zack to his bum. 'I thought I'd lost you!'

'Zack?' it said in a small voice. 'What happened? Where are we?'

'A giant brown blob fell out of the sky,' said Zack. 'That's what happened. And we're trapped inside it.'

'It wasn't my fault!' said Zack's bum. 'I didn't do it! I swear!'

'Calm down,' said Zack. 'I know you didn't.'

'Are we going to die?' said his bum.

'Not if I can help it,' said Zack.

'Great,' said his bum. 'So we ARE going to die!'

Zack was beginning to wish that he hadn't found his bum. He'd forgotten just how annoying it could be.

'I don't want to die!' screamed his bum. 'I'm too young!'

'Then stop complaining and DO something!' said Zack, shaking his bum.

'What?' it said.

'That's exactly what I'm trying to figure out,' said Zack. 'We can keep wiping, but there's no way of telling where we're actually going. We could be going round and round inside this blob forever.'

'Until we die, you mean,' said his bum.

'That's enough!' said Zack. 'You're not helping, you know!'

'Sorry,' said his bum.

But deep down Zack wondered if his bum was right.

He'd wiped and wiped and wiped and there was still no sign of a way out.

'Zack?' said his bum, in a brighter voice. 'Remember when we got caught in the crapalanche?'

'Yes,' said Zack.

'We thought we were going to die then, too, didn't we?' said his bum. 'But we didn't.'

'Actually, we *did*,' said Zack gloomily. 'We went over the Brown river sewagefall. We were crushed to death on the rocks, remember?'

'Oh yeah,' said his bum. 'That's right . . . but that wasn't *real* − it was in the bum-fighting simulator. And we only went over the falls because the Kicker accidentally set the difficulty level on the training program too high. And anyway, what about the brown hole? That *was* real and we got sucked into that and didn't die.'

'I'm not sure about that,' said Zack.

'Not sure about what?' said his bum. 'Not sure that the brown hole was real?'

'No,' said Zack, 'I'm not sure that we survived. I think there's a strong possibility that we died and went to hell . . . *and this is it*!'

'That's not funny, Zack,' said his bum.

'I'm not trying to be funny,' said Zack. 'Even if we do get out, what would be the point? We'll probably just get squashed by another giant brown blob. I thought that after everything we've been through, and everything we've done, the Earth would finally be safe. I was wrong. I now see there's no end to it . . . and there never will be.'

CHAPTER 4

FIGHT!

'So that's it?' said Zack's bum. 'You're giving up?'
'I'm not giving up,' said Zack. 'I'm just accept-ing reality.'

'What about your parents?' said his bum. 'And Eleanor, and Silas Sterne and the Smacker and the Kicker? You're just going to abandon them?'

Zack shrugged. 'I already saved them all,' he said. 'Twice! It's their turn to save me. If they're alive, that is.'

'Zack,' said his bum, 'do you still have the medal and the certificate they gave you at your graduation?'

'Yes,' Zack said.

'You don't deserve them,' said his bum.

'What do you mean?' said Zack. 'I *earned* them.'

'You really believe that?' said his bum. 'You know as well as I do that they only gave them to you because they felt sorry for you.'

'Shut up,' said Zack.

'It's true!' said his bum. 'They all laugh at you

behind your back. Face facts, Zack. You're a total loser. And you always have been. You can't even control me, your own bum, let alone save the world!'

'Do you want an atomic power punch?' said Zack. 'Because you're heading the right way to get one.'

'Oooh, don't scare me,' said his bum.

Despite the pitch-brownness, Zack saw red. Things were bad enough without being taunted by a bum. Especially his own. He was going to teach it some respect, even if it was the last thing he did – which, by the way things were looking, it probably would be. He drew back his fist and let fly.

WHAM!

'Didn't even hurt!' said his bum.

Zack atomic-power-punched it again – this time with both fists.

POW!

The force of the punch sent his bum deep into the brown murk of the blob.

'Call that a double-handed atomic power punch?' said his bum's muffled voice. 'You should be ashamed of yourself. Didn't they teach you anything at the Bum-fighting Academy?'

Zack launched himself forward and set upon his bum with a blood-curdling yell. 'This is all your fault!' he screamed.

Zack punched.

Zack smacked.

Zack kicked.

Zack pinched.

Zack punched and smacked and kicked and

pinched his bum with all the atomic bum-punching bum-smacking bum-kicking bum-pinching force that he could muster.

With every blow they travelled further and further through the blob.

Zack was still punching and smacking and kicking and pinching a few minutes later when he and his bum broke through the thick, dried outer crust of the giant brown blob, and rolled on to the ground.

CHAPTER 5

DIG!

Zack lay on the ground, blinking against the brightness of the day. He was caked with brown blob-sludge. The stench was awful.

'Haven't you two got better things to do than fight at a time like this?' said a voice.

But before Zack could reply – or even stand up – he felt a cold blast of water hit his body. He rolled around on the ground, helpless against the force of the icy torrent.

Finally, just when Zack felt he couldn't possibly get any colder or wetter, the water stopped.

As he lay there shivering, he saw a pair of boots step in front of his face. They were covered in sludge from the blob.

'Well, don't just lie there!' said their owner. 'Get up and give me a hand!'

'Eleanor?' said Zack, wiping water from his eyes.

'No, it's the Easter bunny!' said Eleanor. 'Who do you think?'

'You're not going to hose me again, are you?' said Zack, getting to his knees.

'I will if you don't hurry up,' said Eleanor, still pointing the emergency bum-fighting hose at him. 'Come on! There are people dying in there!'

'But how did *you* get out?' said Zack.

'Anti-giant-brown-blob spray,' said Eleanor, producing a small can from her bum-fighting utility belt. 'I never leave home without it!'

'Nobody told *me* about that,' said Zack.

'You didn't ask,' said Eleanor.

'I didn't even *know* about giant brown blobs!' said Zack.

'Well, you do now,' said Eleanor, waving her hose at the blob in front of them. 'But what you probably *don't* know is that they set hard in less than an hour. We've got to get everybody out before it's too late!'

'He'll be no use,' said Zack's bum, shivering from the same water treatment as Zack had got. 'He's hopeless.'

Zack bent down, picked up his bum and cradled it gently in his arms. 'Shhhh,' he said. 'It's OK. I know you just said all those things to get me mad enough to punch our way out of the blob. But you can stop now. We're out!'

'I meant every word, you bum-fighting wannabe!' said his bum, still punch-drunk from the beating.

'We haven't got time for this!' said Eleanor, thrusting a shovel into Zack's hand. 'You can sort this out later. Meanwhile, we have people to save! Including your mother and father!'

Zack stared at the shovel and felt sick. Compared

to the blob, the shovel seemed no bigger than a teaspoon.

There was no point even starting.

But he couldn't let his parents die!

Not when he was just getting to *really* know them. He'd always believed that they played in the wind section of a symphony orchestra that toured all over the world. He'd had no idea it was a cover for their real work as top secret bum-fighting agents. And he certainly hadn't gone to all the trouble of travelling to Uranus and back to rescue them, just to lose them to a stupid brown blob.

Zack attacked the blob with his shovel.

Eleanor blasted the blob with her hose.

But it was tough going.

After ten minutes Zack was exhausted. The blob seemed to be setting harder with every passing moment. He rested on his shovel, panting. The hole he'd made in the blob was pathetically small. 'It's no use,' he said.

'Keep digging!' said Eleanor. 'We have to try!'

'It's impossible,' said Zack.

'Give me one good reason *why*,' said Eleanor.

'How about that one right behind you?' said Zack's bum.

Zack and Eleanor turned around slowly.

And gasped.

CHAPTER 6

SURROUNDED

There, towering over Zack and Eleanor, was the Great White Bum, the most evil and ruthless bum in the entire history of the world.

Zack felt his heart pounding.

There it stood. Two enormous white cheeks of pure menace – dedicated to nothing less than the downfall of humanity – propped up by two skinny white legs.

'But that's impossible!' whispered Eleanor. 'The Great White Bum was sucked into the brown hole!'

'So were we,' said Zack. 'But you know what? I don't think it *is* the Great White Bum.'

'Of course it is,' said Eleanor. 'I'd know those cheeks anywhere.'

'So would I,' said Zack, 'but those cheeks have no burn marks. No scars. No harpoon wounds.'

'Um, Zack?' said Zack's bum.

'Not now,' said Zack.

'Yes, *right now*!' said Zack's bum. 'Look behind you.'

Hardly daring to take their eyes off the Great White Bum, Zack and Eleanor nevertheless turned around slowly to see something that neither of them could believe.

Another Great White Bum!

'Two Great White Bums?' said Zack, looking from one to the other rapidly. 'But I thought there was only *one.*'

'Three, to be precise,' said Zack's bum, as a shadow passed over them. 'Look to your right.'

Zack and Eleanor, almost beyond shock now, looked to their right. There, sure enough, blocking out the sun, was a third Great White Bum.

Nobody said anything.

They didn't know what *to* say.

Zack's bum broke the silence. 'Actually, better make that four in all,' it said, 'look to your left!'

Zack and Eleanor did not want to look to their left. But look to their left they did, to see a fourth Great White Bum approaching them.

The two bum-fighters now stood back to back and turned slowly as they watched Great White Bums advancing on them from all sides.

The ground was shaking.

Zack's bum leaped into his arms. It was shaking even harder than the ground.

'What do you think this means?' said Zack, trembling in spite of the fact that he was a fully qualified bum-fighter with a special medal for excellence in simulated bum-fighting.

'Well,' said Eleanor, 'I'm just guessing, but I'd say it means we've got a bum-fight on our hands.'

CHAPTER 7

BUM-FIGHT

'You've got to be joking, Eleanor!' said Zack, as the Great White Bums closed in on them. 'We can't possibly fight *four* Great White Bums!'

'Well, what do you suggest we do?' said Eleanor. 'The hokey-cokey?'

'It worked on the zombie bums,' said Zack.

Eleanor rolled her eyes and stepped forward. 'Which one of you is the Great White Bum?' she shouted at the bums.

'Here!' boomed the Great White Bum directly in front of her. 'I'm the Great White Bum.'

'No, I'm greater than you,' said the Great White Bum to her left.

'But I'm the greatest!' said the Great White Bum to her right.

'No, I'm greater than the greatest!' insisted the fourth.

Zack tried to block his nose. The gales of methane emitted as the four Great White Bums argued among themselves were almost worse than the stench of the giant brown blob.

'That's enough!' yelled Eleanor ferociously. 'I'm not in the mood for this.'

The four Great White Bums stopped their argument immediately. Even Zack felt scared. Eleanor was pretty frightening when she was angry. Even if you were a Great White Bum. Even if you were greater than the greatest of the Great White Bums.

'Listen to me,' said Eleanor, turning slowly as she spoke in a low, murderous voice. 'To tell the truth, I don't care which of you is the Great White Bum. What I really want to know is, which one of you is responsible for *this*?'

Eleanor pointed at the giant brown blob.

The four Great White Bums were silent.

'Well?' said Eleanor, her eyes flashing.

'He did it!' said the Great White Bum in front of her, pointing to the one on her left.

'No, I never!' said the accused Great White Bum, turning a deep red and then pointing to the Great White Bum on her right. 'It was him!'

'Liar!' said the Great White Bum on Eleanor's right, pointing to the Great White Bum behind her. 'It was him!'

'No, it wasn't,' said the Great White Bum behind her. 'It was him!'

Eleanor looked at where he was pointing.

It was pointing at Zack's bum.

'How could *I* have done it?' said Zack's trembling bum. 'Look at me! I'm tiny!'

'You are *now*,' said the first Great White Bum. 'Better out than in, I always say.'

The Great White Bum burst out laughing at its little joke. The others joined in.

'Right,' said Eleanor, not impressed. 'That does it. Now you're all going to pay. Zack, you and your bum hit the deck. Now!'

Zack and his bum did as they were instructed.

Eleanor whipped out a Nail-rifle XR-5000 from her bum-fighter's belt, dropped to one knee and spun in a fast circle, spraying the Great White Bums with a double-barrelled burst of six-inch reinforced tungsten-tipped roofing nails.

'Ouch!' said the Great White Bum in front of her.

'Double-ouch!' said the Great White Bum on her left.

'Triple-ouch!' said the Great White Bum on her right.

'Ouch! Ouch! Ouch! Ouch!' said the Great White Bum to her rear.

'Don't you mean "quadruple-ouch"?' said the first Great White Bum.

'I'll be the judge of what I'm feeling,' said the rear bum, letting fly a giant brown blob at the bum in front.

Eleanor and Zack shielded their faces with their hands. SPLAT!

It was a direct hit and pieces of fresh giant brown blob splattered everywhere.

The other Great White Bums laughed.

'Find that funny, do you?' said the freshly hit Great White Bum. 'Well, laugh it up, funny boys!'

And so saying, it launched two giant brown blobs at the giggling bums.

Suddenly the air was alive with giant brown blobs flying in all directions as the four Great White Bums pounded each other in an ear-splitting, nostril-burning free-for-all.

'Come on!' said Zack, putting his bum down and picking up his shovel.

'What are you doing, Zack?' said his bum.

'We've got to get the others out!' said Zack. 'Before it's too late!'

'It already *is* too late,' said Eleanor sadly. 'The blob will have set hard by now.'

'No!' said Zack. 'My parents are in there!'

'I know, Zack,' said Eleanor. 'So is my father. But there's nothing we can do for them now. All we can do is save ourselves and keep fighting. It's what they would have wanted.'

Zack looked at the blob. He looked at Eleanor. He knew she was right, but he still couldn't bring himself to leave.

Eleanor grabbed his arm. 'Get a grip, Zack,' she said, pulling him away.

CHAPTER 8

SCHLOOOMPH!

Zack grabbed his bum and the three of them ran down the hill towards what remained of the Bum-fighting Academy after the Zombie bums' foiled invasion.

Suddenly, all was quiet behind them.

'Uh-oh,' said Zack, turning around. 'I think they've noticed we're missing.'

'How do you know?' said Eleanor.

Zack put out his hand and grabbed Eleanor, bringing her to a dead stop.

'Zack! What do you think you're . . . ?' she started, but then a giant brown blob smashed down right in front of her – right where she would have been if Zack hadn't stopped her.

'Thanks,' said Eleanor.

'No problem,' said Zack.

'Wrong!' said Zack's bum. 'We've got plenty of problems. Look!'

The four Great White Bums had indeed stopped

pounding each other and had turned their attention back to the bum-fighters. Four giant brown blobs were already flying through the air towards them.

SCHLOOOMPH!

A giant brown blob crashed down behind them.

SCHLOOOMPH!

A giant brown blob crashed down in front of them.

'Go left!' yelled Zack.

SCHLOOOMPH!

'Go right!' yelled Zack's bum.

SCHLOOOMPH!

'Don't move!' said Eleanor.

They were surrounded. Again.

Zack, Eleanor and Zack's bum huddled together.

Zack realised it would only be a matter of moments before they were buried beneath a fresh giant brown blob.

He sighed, closed his eyes and blocked his nose.

CHAPTER 9

DEATH RAY

They waited.
And waited.
And waited.
But the blob didn't come.

Zack peered out from between his fingers and looked back up the hill. He couldn't believe what he was seeing. 'Hey!' he whispered to Eleanor and his bum. 'Look!'

The four Great White Bums were still preparing to launch a new round, but now another Great White Bum had flown down out of the sky and landed behind them.

Only this one was even whiter than the others.

The four Great White Bums didn't appear to notice the new bum until it picked two of them up by the top of their cheeks, swung them through the air and smashed them together.

The bums fell limply to the ground.

'Wow!' said Zack's bum. 'That's impressive!'

'Yeah,' said Eleanor. 'But why is it attacking its own kind?'

'Who cares?' said Zack's bum. 'Let's run.'

'Good idea,' said Zack.

The bum-fighters seized their chance. They picked their way through the minefield of brown blobs and ran for the safety of the Bum-fighting Academy dining hall.

After dispatching the other two Great White Bums like the first two, the whitest of the Great White Bums flew down towards the tiny bum-fighters and landed in front of them, blocking their way.

Eleanor drew her nail-rifle. 'Eat six-inch reinforced tungsten-tipped roofing nails!' she yelled, firing off the few remaining rounds. But the nails had no effect. They simply made a metallic pinging sound as they bounced off the bum's shiny white hide.

The Great White Bum just stood there silently.

'I'm out of tricks,' said Eleanor desperately. 'What have you got, Zack?'

'This!' said Zack as he removed his medal and flung it, like a ninja star, at the Great White Bum's left cheek.

But the medal, like Eleanor's nails, bounced harmlessly to the ground.

'That's me out,' said Zack. He turned to his bum. 'You got anything?'

His bum emitted a short burst of gas.

'Pathetic,' said Eleanor. 'But thanks for trying.'

Then the Great White Bum leaned down towards them.

'Nose-pegs on!' said Eleanor. 'It's going to gas us!'

But instead of gassing them, the Great White Bum emitted a dazzling beam of bright white light.

'Aaagghh!' yelled Zack's bum. 'I'm burning up!'

'Me too!' said Zack. 'And I can't move!'

'Me neither!' said Eleanor, trying to cover her eyes with her jacket.

It was as if the light was sucking every bit of energy from their bodies.

So, thought Zack grimly: out of the frying pan and into the fire. They'd escaped from the horror of the brown blob – only to be cooked to a crisp by a Great White Bum's death ray.

Zack tried to shield his eyes from the glare, but as he dragged his arm up to his face he was amazed to see it become transparent and then disappear.

Zack looked down.

His whole body was disappearing.

Right in front of his eyes.

CHAPTER 10

NED

Everything went black.
But only for a moment.
Zack blinked.
And blinked.
And blinked again.

His eyes, still dazzled by the light, slowly adjusted to their new surroundings. Zack saw that he, his bum and Eleanor were standing in exactly the same positions they had been in when they'd been caught in the light.

The only difference was that they were now standing in the centre of a glass cylinder in a room that was filled with computers, levers, pulleys, cogs, springs, dials and wires. There was a bank of security camera-style screens on one wall transmitting grainy black-and-white images. Zack squinted, but was too far away to work out exactly what the images were.

'Teleportation complete,' announced a soothing female voice.

Zack spun around to see who had spoken, but there was nobody there. The voice seemed to come from everywhere and nowhere at the same time.

'Teleported?' said Zack. 'Are we *inside* the Great White Bum?'

'I think so,' said Eleanor, tapping the glass around them with a puzzled look on her face.

'Wow,' said Zack. 'I didn't know Great White Bums had control centres.'

'There's a lot we don't know about Great White Bums,' said Eleanor. 'Including the fact that up to half an hour ago we thought there was only *one* of them. And that we thought we'd seen the last of it.'

'I'm scared,' said Zack's bum, hugging Zack's leg.

'Will you cut that out?!' said Zack.

'But I'm scared!' said Zack's bum.

'No need to be scared!' said a voice from behind them. 'You're with friends now!'

Zack and Eleanor wheeled around.

A bearded man wearing a tattered bum-fighter's uniform and a big smile was standing in front of them.

CHAPTER 11

ROBOBUM

'Ned?' said Zack. The last time Zack had seen Ned was when they were leaving his shack in the Great Windy Desert after he'd helped them to plug up a deadly bumcano. 'Ned Smelly?'

'The very one!' said Ned, stepping forward to slide open the door of the glass tube and embrace his friends. Luckily the terrible body odour that had earned Ned his nickname was no longer evident. Well, at least it was no worse than any other retired bum-fighter's body odour. This was because Ned had given up his diet of needleweeds and stinkants in favour of much less stinky anti-bum energy bars.

The three hugged.

'I came as soon as I could,' said Ned.

'What are you talking about?' said Zack. 'You've been swallowed by a Great White Bum! You have to go where *it* goes!'

Ned laughed. 'Wrong,' he said. 'She goes where I tell her to go. Welcome to *Robobum*!'

Zack looked at Eleanor.

Eleanor looked at Zack.

'Methane madness,' they said in unison.

'No,' said Ned. 'Just a piece of inspired design and a lot of hard work. She's the ultimate bum-fighting machine. I built her out of the parts of crashed and abandoned bum-mobiles I found in the Great Windy Desert.'

'Robobum is a girl?' said Zack's bum. 'Eerrgghh!'

'Yes, well . . .' said Ned. 'It gets lonely out there in the desert. Introduce yourself, Robobum.'

'Hello. I am Robobum,' said the soothing female voice they had heard earlier. 'Fully riveted reinforced steel cheeks. Turbo-assisted jet-repulsion units. Nuclear wart-head equipped. Matter transport assisted entry and exit. Inside and outside voice options. Onboard tea- and coffee-making facilities. And I am self-wiping!'

'Well,' said Ned, proudly. 'What do you think?'

'Is this your idea of a joke?' said Eleanor.

'Joke?' said Ned, a little taken aback. 'What do you mean?'

'Making us think that we were being burned up by a Great White Bum's death ray,' said Eleanor. 'That's what I mean.'

'I'm sorry,' said Ned. 'But I couldn't think how else I could get you inside. Robobum can broadcast her voice outside, but I hardly think you would have accepted an invitation to climb aboard. Please forgive me. And try to look on the bright side: you're now safe inside the ultimate bum-fighting machine. Not only can she travel across land, fly through the air and swim through the sea, she can—'

'Ned,' interrupted Eleanor. 'I'm glad you're so happy with your new toy, but you're too late.'

'What do you mean?' said Ned. 'You're alive, aren't you?'

'Yes,' said Eleanor. 'But everybody else is dead. Half an hour ago a giant brown blob hit the open-air chapel. Everyone was squashed. Zack's parents. My father. The Kicker, the Smacker and this year's entire intake of bum-fighting recruits.'

'We're the only ones who got out alive,' said Zack.

Ned shook his craggy, grizzled head that showed the scars and blast-marks of a lifetime of bum-fighting. 'I'm afraid I have even worse news,' he said softly.

'What could possibly be worse than that?' said Eleanor.

Ned didn't reply. He motioned them to follow him over to the bank of screens flickering on the far wall. 'See for yourself,' he said.

CHAPTER 12

BUMAGEDDON

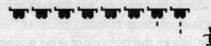

Zack stood in front of the fifty-screen display and blinked. He'd never seen so many television screens at the same time. Or so much destruction.

One screen showed giant brown blobs pounding the pyramids of Egypt into rubble.

Another screen showed a gang of Great White Bums tearing the Eiffel Tower from the ground.

A third screen showed New York being swamped by giant waves of brown sludge.

It was hard for Zack to know which screen to look at.

It was even harder to make sense of the sheer scale of the unfolding disaster. All Zack knew was that it was impossible to look away.

'Zack?' said his bum. 'I'm scared. Can you hold my hand?'

Zack took his bum's trembling hand in his as they watched the unfolding mayhem.

'This is for real?' asked Zack.

'Yes,' said Ned sadly. 'Live via bumcam. Robobum has access to satellites transmitting images from around the world twenty-four hours a day.'

Zack clutched Eleanor's arm. He'd seen isolated towns ravaged by bum attacks before, but nothing on this scale. And he could tell, judging by the expression on Eleanor's face, that neither had she.

Bumquakes. Stink-tornadoes. Brown rain. Crap-alanches. Vast armies of Great White Bums hell-bent on giant-brown-blobbifying the entire world to bumblivion.

'Bumageddon,' whispered Eleanor, as she stared open-mouthed at the nightmarish images on the screens.

CHAPTER 13

BUMAGEDDON?

'**B**umageddon?' said Zack.
    'Bumageddon,' said Ned, nodding solemnly.
'Oh no!' said Zack's bum. 'Not Bumageddon!'
'Yes,' said Eleanor. 'Bumageddon.'

CHAPTER 14

PROPHECY

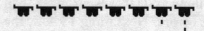

'Well, that's just great,' said Zack. 'Now that we've got that cleared up, would somebody mind telling me what Bumageddon actually is?'

'Affirmative,' crackled Robobum. 'Bumageddon. The complete destruction of the world by bums. As prophesied in the ancient text, *The Book of Bumageddon*, where it is written, "And enormous bums will conquer the world and complete and utter devarsetation will follow. Giant brown blobs will rain down upon the Earth for forty days and forty nights. An evil stench will cover the land. And bums will rule the world again as they did in their glorious prehistoric past."'

Zack gasped. 'Did the ancient texts say anything about how to prevent it?' he said.

Ned shook his head sadly. 'No,' he said. 'They just said it would happen.'

'But how?' said Zack. 'And why? Where did all these Great White Bums come from?'

'That I *do* know,' said Ned. 'Two weeks ago I was in the Great Windy Desert hunting for stinkant juice. Robobum uses it exclusively. It's the most powerful fuel source in the world. A single drop will take you around the world and back – but it's very hard to find. I'd been searching all day without much luck. I was about to head back when I felt a huge tug on the divining rod. It was stronger than anything I'd ever felt before. Next thing I knew, the ground crumbled beneath me and I fell into what turned out to be an ancient stinkant nest. It was huge. I spent the better part of two weeks mapping it before I discovered a tunnel which led me to an enormous cave containing a vast reservoir of prehistoric stinkant juice. I filled my canisters and was about to leave when I noticed something written on the wall.'

Ned paused here, apparently unnerved by the memory.

'What was written on the wall, Ned?' said Eleanor.

Ned pulled a crumpled notepad from his top pocket. 'I wrote it down,' he said. He flipped through the pages, took a deep breath and began to read. '"WARNING! THE GREAT WHITE BUM IS USING THE BROWN HOLE TO SEND PRE-HISTORIC GREAT WHITE BUMS FORWARD THROUGH TIME. STOP HIM OR THE WORLD IS DOOMED."'

Ned closed the pad and put it back into his pocket. 'That's all it said. And underneath there were three skeletons, huddled together.'

Eleanor looked sceptical. 'Are you sure you

weren't suffering methane madness down there?'

'It wasn't methane madness,' said Ned. He reached into his pocket again and pulled out a bar of soap. 'One of the skeletons was holding this.'

Zack looked at the soap and gulped. *Imperial Leather* . . . his grandmother's favourite brand.

CHAPTER 15

SOAP

'Are you all right, Zack?' said Eleanor. 'You've gone all white.'

'That's my . . .' said Zack, finding it difficult to put what he was thinking into words, 'that's my grandmother's soap. You know how fanatical she was about washing her hands.'

Now it was Ned's turn to be confused. 'Your *grandmother's* soap?' he said. 'That's impossible, Zack. I carbon-dated that message. It was sixty-five million years old.'

'Sixty-five million?' said Zack. 'Are you sure?'

'Positive,' said Ned. 'I had Robobum check the results.'

'But that's crazy,' said Zack. 'How could my gran be writing sixty-five-million-year-old messages?'

'Beats me,' said Ned, shrugging.

'Unless . . .' said Eleanor thoughtfully. 'Unless we weren't the only ones who made it out the other end of the brown hole.'

'You think Gran survived as well?' said Zack. 'But we didn't see her on Uranus.'

'Maybe she didn't go to Uranus,' said Eleanor. 'Maybe . . .'

'Hang on,' said Ned, his mouth open in astonishment. 'Are you saying that you got sucked into a brown hole and ended up on Uranus?'

'Yes,' said Eleanor. 'After the zombie bum invasion . . .'

'*Zombie bum invasion?*' said Ned, even more astonished than before.

Eleanor and Zack looked at each other.

'Ned,' said Eleanor, 'how long did you say you were underground in that stinkant nest?'

'About two weeks, I think – I kind of lost track of time,' said Ned, frowning.

'Did you have any contact with the outside world while you were down there?' said Zack. 'Radio? Bumcam?'

'Nothing,' said Ned. 'I was too far underground. What on earth happened?'

'It's a long story,'* said Zack, 'but after the Great White Bum was blown out of the bumcano last month, he was flung through space and collided with Uranus. The collision created a huge explosion that caused a whole load of bums to turn into zombies, which then attacked the Earth. We fought them off, but ended up chasing the Great White Bum back into outer space, where we were sucked into a brown hole, along with a load of giant mutant zombie

*For the full story see *Zombie Bums from Uranus,* Andy Griffiths.

blowflies, my gran – the Pincher – and two other bum-fighters, the Flicker and the Forker. We didn't know what had happened to them. Until now, that is.'

'Let me get this straight,' said Ned. 'Are you saying that one of those skeletons might have been your gran?'

'It would certainly explain the soap,' said Eleanor. 'And the message. The brown hole must have sucked her, the other bum-fighters and the Great White Bum back to prehistoric times – when prehistoric bumosaurs ruled the Earth!'

'So you think the Great White Bum is using the brown hole as some sort of bridge from the past to the present?' said Zack's bum.

'It's possible,' said Eleanor. 'And not just *the* Great White Bum. *All* of the Great White Bums.'

'But why?' said Zack. 'Why doesn't he just stay there with all his pals?'

'Ah,' said Ned. 'I think I can answer that one. If my – and Robobum's – calculations are correct, that message was written just before a very important event in the Earth's history. Less than twenty-four hours after that message was written, a giant arseteroid slammed into the Earth and caused the extinction of all the bumosaurs, including the prehistoric Great White Bums.'

'And my gran,' said Zack, stunned.

'And your gran,' said Ned.

CHAPTER 16

REWIND

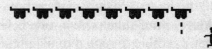

Zack felt dizzy as he tried to make sense of Ned's words.

'So, let me get this straight,' said Eleanor, frowning. 'The Great White Bum is actually a Great White Bumosaur, a relic from the times when Great White Bumosaurs ruled the Earth.'

'Correct,' said Ned.

'And in the original history of the Earth all of the Great White Bumosaurs – except for the Great White Bum for some reason – were wiped out when a giant arseteroid hit the Earth.'

'Correct again,' said Ned.

'But now, the Great White Bum has taken advantage of the brown hole's closeness to the Earth to provide an escape route from the doomed past to the safety of the present.'

'Exactly,' said Ned.

'So the answer is simple,' said Eleanor.

'It is?' said Zack's bum.

'Yes,' said Eleanor. 'We have to go back in time and stop the Great White Bum from carrying out its evacuation.'

'But how?' said Zack.

'I'll spell it out for you,' said Eleanor. 'We go back to the past. We use Robobum's nuclear wart-head to terminate the Great White Bum once and for all — before he puts his plan into action. Without the Great White Bum's help, the other Great White Bums won't be able to return to the present. They'll die – as they did, and as they should have done – when the arseteroid hits. Meanwhile, we'll return to the present . . . a *Great White Bum-free* present.'

Zack gulped as he realised what Eleanor was proposing. 'But that's dangerous,' he said.

'So is staying here, in case you hadn't noticed,' said Eleanor.

'But brown holes are unpredictable,' said Zack. 'We went into the same brown hole as the rest of them and we didn't go back into the past. What makes you think that it will work this time?'

'There's a better—' started Ned, but he was cut off by Eleanor.

'Let me handle him,' said Eleanor. 'He's a bit slow.'

'I am *not* slow!' said Zack.

'You are,' said his bum.

'Thanks for your support,' said Zack. 'You're sup-posed to be on my side.'

'On your backside to be exact,' said his bum.

'I wish,' said Zack. Then he turned back to Eleanor. 'All I'm saying is what your father told us, over and over. They are *too dangerous*. And besides, my mum made me *promise*.'

Tears filled Eleanor's eyes. 'Zack,' she said slowly, 'neither your mum nor my dad is alive any more. Promises made back then don't count. Neither do warnings. That was another world ago. Things have changed, and we have to adapt or we could very well end up extinct ourselves.'

Zack was silent.

'Besides,' said Eleanor, 'we owe it to their memory to try to stop this. It's what they would have wanted us to do, no matter how dangerous.' She paused. 'It's what they would do – if they could.'

Zack looked at the sickening images on the screens.

He knew Eleanor was right, but he was still terrified.

'There is another way,' said Ned.

'Another way?' said Eleanor. 'What are you talking about?'

CHAPTER 17

PREPARATIONS

'Well,' said Ned, 'apart from her other features, Robobum is fully equipped for time travel.'

'Why didn't you say so?' said Eleanor.

'I've been trying to,' said Ned. 'But you wouldn't let me.'

'Time travel?' said Zack. 'But don't you need a . . .'

'Perambulic merimbulator?' said Ned.

'Yes!' said Zack, who'd studied time-machine technology for a school project.

'I've got one,' said Ned. 'Robobum instructed me how to make a rudimentary one out of a tin and an old mattress spring.'

'Brilliant!' said Zack. 'And it can go all the way back? Sixty-five million years?'

'Yes,' said Ned. 'At least, I think so.'

'What do you mean, you THINK so?' said Eleanor.

'Well,' said Ned, 'I've never actually tested it. I've

been too busy. But you know what they say about time travel? There's no time like the present!'

Zack rolled his eyes at Ned's joke.

'Well, what are we waiting for?' said Eleanor. 'Let's do it!'

'Right you are,' said Ned. 'Robobum . . . prepare for time travel!'

'Affirmative,' said Robobum. 'Please enter the passenger pods and secure safety harnesses. I will then present a short film about time-travel safety.'

'Skip the safety presentation,' said Ned. 'We have to get out of here before we end up Bumageddonised ourselves. We've got a human race to save.'

'Understood,' said Robobum. 'Safety presentation suspended. But please exercise extreme caution at all times. Even the tiniest change to the past may have catastrophic effects on the future.'

'Warning heard and understood,' said Ned. He led Zack, Zack's bum and Eleanor over to a bank of what looked like six glass coffins.

'Well, whatever we do,' said Zack's bum as it lay down in one of the pods, 'it can't be any worse than what's already happening.'

'The small bum speaks the truth,' said Robobum.

CHAPTER 18

COUNTDOWN

'Time travel commencing in T-minus twenty seconds,' announced Robobum.

Zack took a deep breath as he climbed into his pod. His stomach was churning. They were about to voyage sixty-five million years into the past on the most important bum-fighting mission ever under-taken in the entire history of bum-fighting.

The world – as they'd known it – was doomed.

Bumageddon was nigh.

'Time travel commencing in T-minus fifteen sec-onds,' announced Robobum.

Zack looked at Ned, who was adjusting the dials on the temporal navigator – a dome-like structure that allowed them to control both the direction and the distance of their passage through time.

'Time travel commencing in T-minus ten sec-onds,' announced Robobum.

At last Ned finished setting their course. He walked up to his pod, climbed inside and strapped himself in. He signalled to Zack to do the same.

'Time travel commencing in T-minus five seconds,' announced Robobum. 'Five . . .'

Zack fumbled with his belt.

'Four . . .'

'Stupid belt!' said Zack.

'Three . . .'

'Great!' he said. 'Most important mission ever, and no safety belt!'

'Two . . .'

Zack clutched the handgrips on his pod as tightly as he could.

'One . . .'

Zack closed his eyes.

CHAPTER 19

650,000,000 BC

Zack held his breath and waited . . . but nothing seemed to happen. He opened his eyes. 'When do we leave?' he said.

'We're already there!' said Ned, climbing out of his pod.

'What do you mean?' said Eleanor, sitting up. 'It didn't feel like we moved at all.'

'No,' said Ned. 'Technically speaking, we didn't move. Time moved through us.'

'Huh?' said Eleanor, frowning.

'We must have moved *somewhere*,' said Zack, standing in front of the bumcam monitors. 'Look!'

Eleanor, Ned and Zack's bum came over and joined Zack at the screens.

Bumcam now consisted of a single super-sized image provided by a hidden camera mounted on the top of Robobum.

They were looking at a small inlet with a range of rocky, treeless mountains in the distance. Robobum was sitting in the middle of a large stretch of feature-less mudflats.

Apart from a strong wind that buffeted Robobum's riveted steel panels, there was nothing but mudflats and water and smoking bumcanoes for as far as they could see.

There was no sign of life.

No animals.

No people.

No bums.

Nothing.

'Where are we?' said Zack's bum.

'I don't know,' said Eleanor, 'but if this is sixty-five million BC, where are all the bumosaurs? There's not a lot of action out there.'

'No,' said Ned, looking a little worried as he bent over his temporal navigator. 'I think I might have made a slight miscalculation.'

'How much of a slight miscalculation?' said Eleanor.

'Well,' said Ned, 'instead of going back sixty-five million years, we've gone back *six hundred and fifty* million years.'

CHAPTER 20

MUD

'Six hundred and fifty million years!' spluttered Eleanor. 'That is not a slight miscalculation, Ned. That is a miscalculation of major proportions!'

'It's only an extra zero,' said Ned.

'That extra zero makes a big difference!' said Eleanor. 'Five hundred and eighty-five million years' worth of difference, to be exact.'

'I told you Robobum's time-travel capabilities hadn't been tested,' said Ned, sheepishly. 'There must be a loose screw in the temporal navigator.'

'I think I know where the loose screw is,' said Eleanor. 'It's—'

'Take it easy, Eleanor,' said Zack. 'I'm sure Ned's doing his best.'

'Well, this is just great, isn't it?' said Eleanor. 'While Ned tinkers with his time-travel toy, the Earth is being Bumageddonised and we're five hundred and eighty-five million years away from being able to do anything about it.'

'That's not technically correct,' said Zack. 'The Earth isn't in any immediate danger of Bumageddon . . . it's not going to happen for another six hundred and fifty million years. Ned's got plenty of time to figure it out.'

'Oh, well, that's all right, then,' said Eleanor. 'In the meantime we might just as well relax and have a holiday. Anyone for a swim?'

'I wouldn't do that if I were you,' said Zack's bum, who had been busy gazing at the screen all this time. 'There's something moving out there.'

'Impossible,' said Robobum. 'Oxygen levels are too low to sustain advanced life forms.'

'But there's something moving!' insisted Zack's bum. 'Look, there, just at the water's edge.'

'Move in for a closer look, Robobum,' said Ned.

With a barely audible sigh, Robobum slowly moved forward. As she did so, the bum-fighters were amazed to see movement in the mud. There was a small shape wriggling on the surface.

'That's close enough, Robobum,' said Ned. 'Whatever it is, we don't want to alarm it.'

'I hate to say I told you so,' said Zack's bum, 'but I told you so.'

'I stand corrected,' said Robobum. 'We are witnessing one of the earliest, most primitive forms of life on the planet.'

'What is it?' said Zack.

'I do not know,' said Robobum. 'Insufficient data.'

'We can fix that,' said Eleanor. In an instant she had been transformed from a frustrated bum-fighter into an eager scientist. She grabbed one of the extra-vehicular bum-fighting suits hanging up next to the teleportation tube.

'What are you doing, Eleanor?' said Zack.

'You heard Robobum,' said Eleanor. 'She needs data. I'm going out to take a closer look. Six hundred and fifty million years takes us right into the heart of the geological period known as the Pre-Cambrian. There are not a whole lot of fossils dating back this far – and it's not like we'll be here again. It's too good an opportunity to miss. The more data that Robobum – and we – have, the better our chances of success.'

'If you survive long enough to gather the data, that is,' said Ned. 'I wouldn't leave the ship if I were you.'

'Yeah?' said Eleanor. 'Well, you're not me, Ned. Besides, how dangerous can it be out there? It's got to be a lot safer than where we just came from.'

'I suppose I'd better come with you, then,' sighed Zack. He knew it was no use arguing with Eleanor.

'Which means I'll have to come, to look after you both,' said Zack's bum.

Zack smiled. 'Thanks,' he said. 'I knew I could count on you. Ned?'

Ned was already climbing into his suit. 'If you think I'm going to let you crazy kids go out there on your own, you need your heads read. Robobum – you're in charge. If there's any sign of trouble I want you to beam us up straight away.'

'Affirmative,' said Robobum.

CHAPTER 21

BUMOLUTION

A strong wind greeted the bum-fighters as they teleported on to the grey sludge of prehistoric Earth. They leaned into the squall and began squelching across the ancient mudflats.

'Can I ride on your shoulder, Zack?' said his bum. 'I'm tired.'

'But we've only just started,' said Zack. 'How can you be tired?'

'My legs aren't as big – or as strong – as yours,' it said.

'OK,' said Zack, bending down. 'Climb aboard.'

'It's amazing,' said Eleanor. 'The whole Earth. All new. Completely unspoilt.'

'I wouldn't be so sure of that,' said Ned.

'Why?' said Zack.

'Our friend in the mud there,' said Ned, pointing. 'See the little crease running from top to bottom? If I didn't know better, I'd say it was a . . . bum.'

As they closed in on it, Eleanor put out her arm to

stop Zack and Ned. 'Slowly and quietly,' she said. 'Let's not disturb it unnecessarily. It doesn't look dangerous, but you never know.'

They nodded and moved the last few metres towards the primitive life form in silence.

At first glance Zack thought it was a jellyfish. Then, when he looked closer, it appeared to be *two* jellyfish, but without tentacles, just four stumpy little protuberances. And then, like a magic 3D picture coming into focus, the two jellyfish globes merged into one single organism and Zack realised what he was actually looking at. The two halves were joined with a crevice running through the middle. Ned was right. It was a bum. Primitive and barely formed, but unmistakably a bum.

Eleanor let out a long breath. 'So, Sir Roger Francis Rectum was right,' she said.

'About what?' said Zack.

'Bumolution!' she said. 'His theory was that the first life forms were bums. Look – you can see the little stumps that will one day be arms and legs. Sir Roger was ridiculed for his beliefs by the scientific community of his time, but he was right. We evolved from bums, Zack.'

'I like that theory!' said Zack's bum.

'It's not a theory any more,' said Eleanor. 'It's now an official fact. At least it will be, once I've taken a photograph.'

'I wouldn't do that if I were you,' said Ned. 'The flash might disturb it.'

'I don't think so,' said Eleanor. 'A life form this primitive won't have any visual receptors. They don't evolve for at least another hundred million years.'

Before Ned could stop her, Eleanor took a small camera out of her pocket and took a photo, bathing the primeval bum in a momentary flash of bright white light.

CHAPTER 22
HATCH

The reaction was instant.

The bum flipped up and over on to its back, its stumps wiggling crazily.

'Stand back!' said Ned. 'It may not have an eye, but it's got heat sensors.'

The bum-fighters gave the bum a wide berth as it continued its agonised flipping. But as it flipped, it revealed that it was protecting a small clutch of white eggs. And whether it was due to the flipping of the bum, the heat of the camera's flash, or whether it was just the right time to do so, they were beginning to hatch.

The bum-fighters stood and watched in wonder as dozens of the eggs cracked open and a clutch of tiny jelly-like bums emerged. All except one, which, unlike its brothers and sisters, was not see-through jelly, but a pure gleaming white.

'Look at that!' said Zack. 'It's a mutant!'

Eleanor clutched his arm. 'It's *white*, Zack,' she said. 'Do you realise what we're looking at?'

'Yes,' said Zack, 'a mutant. That's how bumo-lution works, isn't it? Little mutations to the basic patterns that give an organism an advantage – or a disadvantage, as the case may be.'

'Definitely a disadvantage in this case,' said Ned.

'I don't understand,' said Zack.

'Gee, you can be thick, Zack,' said Eleanor. *'It's the Great White Bum!'*

'I think that's jumping to conclusions, isn't it?' said Zack. 'Out of all the primeval mudflats in all the possible years that we could have landed in, we touch down right in the exact spot at the exact time that the Great White Bum is being hatched? You've got to be joking!'

But a glance at the terrified faces of his companions told Zack that he was in the minority on this one.

'Stranger things have happened,' said Eleanor.

Not many, thought Zack, as he stared at the small white bum. And then an idea began to form in his mind.

An idea so huge that he could hardly contain it in his head.

An idea so daring that only one bum-fighter on the planet could possibly have conceived it, let alone considered it.

What if, he thought, what if I killed the Great White Bum right now? Killed it in the nest. Killed it before it had a chance to grow up and do all the evil that it was going to do. There would be no enormous bumcanoes – filled with bums loyal to the Great White Bum – capable of gassing the entire world. No zombie bum invasions.

And, most important of all, no Bumageddon.

Of course, there would be no such thing as bum-fighters, either, but Zack realised this was not about him.

This was bigger than all of them.

This was about the future of the entire world.

Hadn't the Blind Bum-feeler predicted this?

Hadn't she told him that he would be the saviour of free men everywhere . . . past, present and future?

To what else, apart from this moment, could she possibly have been referring?

Zack put his bum down on the ground. He drew his bum-gun from his bum-fighting utility belt and raised it to his shoulder.

CHAPTER 23

EXTERMINATE!

'Zack!' yelled Eleanor. 'What do you think you're doing?'

'We have to kill it,' said Zack.

'No!' said Ned.

'What do you mean, "no"?' said Zack. 'One shot now could prevent a lot of suffering and save millions of lives in the future. It's the Great White Bum. Or at least its father. Or its father's father.'

'Or its father's father's father,' said Zack's bum helpfully.

'Whatever,' said Zack. 'I have to kill it. Now. While there's still time.'

'But it hasn't done anything wrong,' said Ned. 'Not yet. You would be killing an innocent bum.'

'But it's not going to *stay* innocent!' said Zack. 'We *know* that! That's why we're here!'

'No,' said Ned. 'That's *not* why we're here. We came back for one reason and one reason only: to prevent the Great White Bum from sending prehistoric

Great White Bums into the future and upsetting the natural bumolution of the planet. We didn't come to strip it – or any other carbon-based life form – of its right to life in the first place. I don't like the idea of bum rebellion or bumcanoes or zombie bums any more than you do, but if we kill it now we'll be no better than the Great White Bum himself.'

'Great White Bums killed my parents, Ned,' said Zack. 'Great White Bums killed your parents, Eleanor. And they destroyed our planet. Doesn't that count for anything?'

'Of course it does, Zack,' said Ned. 'But it doesn't change the fact that this is not our decision to make.'

'If it's not ours, then whose is it?' said Zack.

'Nobody's!' said Ned. 'It's too big a change. OK, you might get rid of the Great White Bum, but there's no telling what else you might change – or create – in the process. You might create the conditions for the emergence of a monster that makes the Great White Bum look as harmless as a pussy cat! Don't try to play God, Zack.'

'I never said I was God,' said Zack. 'I'm just a bum-fighter and I've got a bum to fight.'

'I agree with Ned,' said Eleanor. 'I don't like the Great White Bum any more than you do, but two wrongs don't make a right.'

'True,' said Zack. 'But a stitch in time saves nine. How many more people have to die? How many more planets have to be destroyed before we take action?'

'That's enough,' said Ned. 'I order you to put your gun down immediately, Zack. I can see why you want to do what you want to do, but you could be introducing catastrophic time-travel errors which I cannot allow myself – or any of us – to be responsible for.'

Zack was silent.

'Zack?' said Ned. 'Did you hear me? I gave you a direct order!'

'I'm sorry, Ned,' said Zack. 'I cannot obey that order.'

'Fine,' said Ned, lunging towards Zack. 'Then I'll obey it for you!'

Zack watched Ned as he sailed towards him, as if in slow motion.

Ned's heavy body knocked Zack sideways.

But not before Zack's shaking finger had squeezed the bum-gun trigger.

As Zack fell, a volley of bum-gun bullets sprayed the nest. The newly hatched bums – at least, the ones that weren't hit by the bullets – scattered like a flock of startled birds.

'You idiot, Zack!' yelled Eleanor. 'Now look what you've done!'

Zack ignored Eleanor, jumped to his feet and kept shooting until all the bums lay dead in the mud.

Well, *almost* all of them. All except for the white one.

'Zack!' said his bum. 'It's still alive!'

'Where is it?' yelled Zack. 'Where did it go?'

'Over there!' said his bum, pointing.

Zack turned.

The mutant hatchling had already moved just out of range.

Zack squelched through the slime after it, shooting all the while.

But it was fast.

And agile.

Zack's bullets hit the mud and the water around the bum as it rolled first one way and then the other.

As much as Zack hated the Great White Bum, he had to admire it. Even at this early age it was already clearly a survivor.

And even as he had this thought, the hatchling flew into the air and took off into the sky.

Whether it was the first time in the history of the Earth that a bum had left the safety of the mud and taken to the air, Zack had no way of knowing. But he wasn't about to let it get away.

'Robobum!' Zack yelled at the top of his voice. 'Hurry!'

CHAPTER 24

BUM HUNT

But Robobum was already in the air.
Even before Zack had finished speaking he was engulfed by Robobum's matter-transporting beam. In an instant he found himself sprawled on the control room floor, along with Ned, Eleanor and his bum.

'Follow that bum!' said Zack, picking himself up and rushing to the viewing screens.

'Affirmative,' said Robobum. 'Tracking system locked on. Hold tight.'

Zack grabbed the temporal navigator to keep from falling backwards as Robobum shot up into the air.

The sky was beginning to turn from blue to black as Robobum flew higher and higher in pursuit.

'Ned!' said Eleanor. 'We're leaving the atmosphere!'

'Don't worry,' said Ned. 'Robobum is space-travel ready and full of stinkant juice. We can go anywhere. But I'm not sure this is such a good idea.'

'We've got to finish what we started,' said Zack.

'What *you* started,' said Eleanor.

'Maybe we should just let it go,' said Zack's bum.

'No,' said Zack, his eyes burning. 'We have to do whatever it takes. Go wherever we need to go. This is the most important bum hunt in history! If we can catch this bum, there won't be any need for anyone to catch a bum ever again. Without the Great White Bum inciting bums to rebellion, bums across the univarse will be able to work *with* their bodies instead of against them.'

'But *I* work with you,' said Zack's bum.

'*Now* you do,' said Zack. 'But it hasn't always been that way, has it?'

Before Zack's bum could reply, Robobum suddenly turned steeply.

'Changing course,' said Robobum.

'Ouch!' said Zack as he lost his grip on the navigator and fell, face first, against the bumcam screens. The other bum-fighters fell right on top of him, powerless to resist the intense B-forces unleashed by the dive. Zack could see that the tiny white bum was now heading back towards the ground. But not for long.

Zack was close to blacking out when Robobum changed course again. This time the bum-fighters fell hard against the back wall.

Then Robobum changed course again.

And again.

And yet again.

The bum-fighters were being thrown around like dirty socks in a washing machine.

Zack felt his head smash against something hard.

There was a huge crash.
And then silence.

CHAPTER 25

65,000,000 BC

'OUCH!' said Robobum. 'That hurt!'
Inside Robobum, her hapless occupants lay
on the floor and blinked stupidly at one another.

They tried to remember who they were.

They tried to remember where they were.

They tried to remember why they were where they
were.

Zack's bum was the first to fully reorient
itself.

'Zack!' it said, jumping on to his lap. 'Wake up!'

Zack looked at his bum dumbly.

'Pleased to meet you,' he said, extending his hand.
'My name is Zack.'

'I know who you are!' said his bum, slapping Zack's
hand away. 'It's me – your bum – remember?'

Zack tried to focus on the small pink excitable bum
in front of him. It looked familiar, but he was having
a lot of trouble remembering why.

'You look like somebody I know . . .' said Zack.

'Maybe this will jog your memory,' said his bum, farting in Zack's face.

The obnoxious odour sent Zack into a doubled-over coughing fit, but when he'd come to, he remembered exactly who he was. And exactly who *it* was.

'Why, you . . .' he said to his bum, reaching out to strangle it.

'Steady, Zack,' it said, jumping out of the way. 'You were delirious. I had to do it. I'm sorry.'

'Not as sorry as I am,' said Zack, stifling another coughing fit. Beside him, Eleanor and Ned were coughing and returning to their senses as well.

Zack rose to his feet – a little dizzy from both the foul air and the blow to his head. He staggered to the bumcam screens.

He could see that they were in a lush bumnut-tree forest. The bumnut trees were enormous – taller than any he had ever seen – their thick brown fronds blocking out the sky.

'I don't believe it,' said Ned from behind him. 'I don't believe it!'

'What?' said Zack.

Ned was bent over the temporal navigator. 'I don't know how this has happened, but the temporal navigator indicates that we are deep in the heart of the late Cretaceous period.'

'What does that mean?' said Zack's bum.

'It's sixty-five million years BC,' said Ned, still shaking his head in wonder.

'You mean we just travelled through time?' said Eleanor. 'Forward?'

'It would seem so,' said Ned, scratching his beard.

'It appears that we're exactly where we need to be.'

'Thanks, Ned!' said Eleanor. 'You're a genius!'

'I didn't do anything,' said Ned. 'Thank Robobum!'

'Thanks, Robobum,' said Eleanor.

'I cannot take credit for this outcome,' said Robobum. 'Thank Zack.'

'Me?' said Zack, rubbing his head. 'What did I do?'

'When you fell, your head hit the temporal navigator control panel,' said Robobum. 'The force not only initiated time travel, but at the same time fixed the loose screw that caused the 585-million-year error on our last trip.'

'I did all that?' said Zack, proudly.

'It was the *least* you could do,' said Eleanor.

'What do you mean?' said Zack.

'You know exactly what I mean,' said Eleanor. 'It was the least you could do to make up for the botched attempt to kill the Great White Bum.'

'At least I tried,' said Zack. 'Better to try and fail than never to have tried at all.'

'No,' said Eleanor. 'Not in this case. In this case it was better *not* to try than to fail. You just made an enemy of the Great White Bum.'

'What are you talking about?' said Zack. 'He wasn't exactly our friend to begin with!'

'No,' she said. 'Because you tried to kill him.'

'You've been trying to kill him for a lot longer than I have,' said Zack.

'Oh, really?' said Eleanor. 'I seem to remember that it was *you* who fired the first-ever shot at him.'

'Huh?' said Zack.

'Five hundred and eighty-five million years ago,' said Eleanor. 'And if my memory serves me correctly, I also seem to remember that you *missed*.'

'Ned dived on me,' said Zack.

'I was just trying to stop you from creating a bigger problem than we already had,' said Ned.

'What could be bigger than Bumageddon?' said Zack.

'Bumageddon didn't exist at that moment,' said Ned. 'You were way out of line and way off mission. You might have killed the Great White Bum, yes, but by doing so, you might also have completely altered the course of bumolution and erased the possibility of humans even evolving.'

'Would that have been such a bad thing?' said Zack's bum.

The bum-fighters all turned and glared at Zack's bum.

'Just joking,' it said quickly.

'I was only trying to do what I thought was best,' said Zack quietly.

'Yeah, well, no more heroics,' said Eleanor. 'You might have a certificate and a medal, but bum-fighting is a team effort, and the sooner you realise that, the better.'

Zack nodded dejectedly.

Maybe she was right.

Suddenly the silence of the forest was broken by a horrendous howl. The ground began to shake around them.

'What's that?' said Zack's bum, as the howl

sounded again, even closer this time.

'I don't know,' said Zack. 'But whatever it is, it sounds like it's in pain.'

'Robobum!' said Ned. 'Can you identify what is making that sound?'

'Insufficient data,' said Robobum.

Ned stood up and started rifling through a collection of books on an overhead shelf. He selected a thick volume called *What Bumosaur is That?* and began quickly leafing through the pages. 'Uh-oh,' he said. 'If I didn't know better, I'd say that's the sound of a tyrannosore-arse . . .'

'And here it is!' said Eleanor, as the image of an enormous, throbbing red bum, its cheeks lined with two rows of huge, sharp, dagger-like teeth, appeared on the screens and began charging towards them.

CHAPTER 26

TYRANNOSORE-ARSE

Zack stared at the bumcam screens. He had seen some terrifying and unpleasant sights in his short career as a bum-fighter, but few as terrifying – or as unpleasant – as this.

'What are you waiting for, Ned?' said Eleanor. 'Get this hunk of tin moving!'

'Robobum is not a hunk of tin,' said Robobum. 'I am Robobum. Fully riveted reinforced steel cheeks. Turbo-assisted jet-repulsion units. Nuclear wart-head equipped. Matter transport assisted entry and exit. Inside and outside voice options. Onboard tea- and coffee-making facilities. And I am self-wiping!'

'Spare us the details,' said Eleanor. 'Just run!'

'Unable to run,' said Robobum. 'Currently per-forming damage assessment.'

'No time for that now!' said Ned. 'Move!'

But it was already too late.

Zack stared, transfixed and sickened, as the tyrannosore-arse cheek-butted Robobum and sent her flying through the bumnut-tree forest.

Zack, Eleanor, Ned and Zack's bum were thrown violently from one side of Robobum to the other. They landed heavily on top of each other as Robobum came to rest, wedged between two bumnut trees.

'Do you think it's finished with us?' said Zack.

There was another howl and then the ground started to shake again.

'I suspect it's only just begun,' said Ned, looking up from his guidebook. 'It says here that the tyranno-sore-arse likes to play with its food . . . before eating it.'

Through the upside-down bumcam of Robobum, they could see the tyrannosore-arse crashing towards them again.

'If this is playing, then I'd hate to see it when it gets serious,' said Zack's bum.

'Me too,' said Eleanor. 'Switch to manual control, Ned!'

'Good idea,' said Ned.

'Bad idea!' said Robobum. 'Strongly recom—'

Robobum's voice was shut off mid-sentence as Ned pulled down on a lever.

'Done,' said Ned.

'Then what are we waiting for?' said Eleanor. 'Go!'

'I'm trying,' said Ned, 'but we're wedged between the trees!'

'Hurry!' said Zack, watching as the enraged tyrannosore-arse opened its cheeks again and clamped them down hard over the top of Robobum.

Everything went d... for a second...
felt Robobum being lifte...

'That's got it!' said Ned.

Suddenly the room was fille...
tyrannosore-arse hurled Robobum ...
once more.

This time, however, Ned was able to a...
Robobum's 'flight' program and they hit the for...
floor running.

'Good going, Ned,' said Eleanor as Robobum
dodged bumnut trees and leaped over rivers and
bogs.

'It's still chasing us!' said Zack, listening to the
loud, outraged howls close behind them.

'Relax!' said Ned. 'This is just a walk in the
park for Robobum. Wait till I really get this baby
going.'

'I wouldn't do that if I were you,' said Eleanor,
placing her hand on Ned's to stop him opening the
throttle.

'Why not?' he said.

'Look,' said Eleanor, her eyes wide.

CHAPTER 27

RUN!

Directly in front of Robobum was another tyrannosore-arse, even bigger than the one chasing them. And not only was it bigger, it was redder. And louder. It pawed the forest floor angrily, howled and charged towards them.

Ned didn't hesitate.

He pushed the emergency stop button, sending them all piling towards the bumcam screens.

'What do we do now?' said Eleanor.

'I don't know,' said Ned.

'Ned, I think it's time to put Robobum back in control of herself,' said Zack. 'Maybe she will have had time to figure out what to do.'

'Can't hurt,' said Ned, throwing the switch back to automatic.

'Hello, I am Robobum,' said Robobum, crackling back to life. 'Fully riveted reinforced steel cheeks. Turbo-assisted jet repulsion units. Nuclear wart-head equipped. Matter transport assisted entry and

72

exit. Inside and out
tea- and coffee-making
wiping!'

'Robobum!' said Ned. 'I kn
remember? It's Ned! Ned Smelly!'

'I know who you are,' said Robobum. 'I
me off. Don't do that again.'

'Sorry,' said Ned. 'But you've got to help u..
We're being attacked by two tyrannosore-arses. What
should we do?'

'Leave them to me,' announced Robobum. 'Meanwhile, I advise you to abandon ship immediately! It's
going to get rough. Too rough for passengers. I'll
pick you up later.'

Zack, Ned, Eleanor and Zack's bum didn't argue.
They assembled in the teleportation tube and beamed
themselves clear of Robobum only moments before
the two tyrannosore-arses closed in.

'Ned!' said Robobum, in her loudest outside voice.
'You forgot this!'

Robobum beamed Ned's copy of *What Bumosaur
is That?* into his hand.

'Thanks, Robobum!' cried Ned. 'Be careful!'

'Do not concern yourself about me,' she said. 'I
am Robobum. Fully riveted reinforced steel cheeks.
Turbo-assisted jet-repulsion units. Nuclear wart-
head equipped. Matter transport assisted entry and
exit. Inside and outside voice options. Onboard tea-
and coffee-making facilities. And I am self-wiping! I
am perfectly capable of handling myself.'

'Come on, Ned,' said Eleanor, trying to drag him
away from Robobum.

'...they're going to destroy her!' said Ned. 'My baby!'

'They'll destroy us if we don't find a place to hide,' said Eleanor, grabbing Ned and dragging him into the thick undergrowth.

CHAPTER 28

TRICERABUTT

The bum-fighters fought their way through the shaded semi-tropical undergrowth. Zack wiped his sweating brow and marvelled at the difference that 585 million years can make. The Earth had come alive. There were bumnut-tree forests in place of grey sludge. Giant mutant blowflies droned around their heads. Enormous red stinkants lumbered in single file across the forest floor. And, of course, terrifying bumosaurs ruled the planet.

As they hacked through thick vines and even thicker spider webs, the bum-fighters could hear Robobum preparing to do battle with the tyrannosore-arses.

'I must warn you,' said Robobum, 'I have fully riveted reinforced steel cheeks. Turbo-assisted jet-repulsion units . . .'

There was a loud tyrannosore-arse howl.

A sickening metallic crunch.

And then . . . silence.

Zack glanced back at Ned.

Ned looked at Zack.

'Nuclear wart-head equipped,' said a voice. 'Matter transport assisted entry and exit. Inside and outside voice options. Onboard tea- and coffee-making . . .'

The bum-fighters grinned with relief. But not for long.

There was another howl.

Followed by another crunch.

Silence.

And then . . .

'. . . and I am self-wiping!'

A third crunch.

And a fourth.

And a fifth.

Ned put his hands over his ears. 'Robobum!' he cried. 'My Robobum!'

'Come on, Ned,' said Eleanor, putting her arm around his shoulders. 'We have to look after our-selves now. It's what Robobum would want.'

Zack, who was leading, pushed his way into a rectan-gular clearing that was about the size of a soccer pitch.

'Hey!' said his bum, trying to brighten the mood. 'Anyone for soccer?'

'We don't have a ball,' said Ned.

'We could use Zack's bum,' said Eleanor.

'Not funny!' said Zack's bum.

They were halfway across the clearing when Zack screamed.

'Shut up!' said Eleanor. 'Do you want the tyrannosore-arses to hear us?'

'No,' said Zack. 'But . . .'

'But what?' said Eleanor.

Zack was speechless.

He could only point.

Charging towards them was a huge armoured bum with three cheeks. Each cheek had a large wart in its centre.

And each wart was sharpened to a deadly point.

'Oh no,' said Ned, looking from his guidebook to the bumosaur and then back to the book. 'A tricerabutt!'

'We can see that!' said Zack's bum. 'How do you stop it?'

'You can't,' said Ned, consulting his book. 'It says here that nothing can stop a charging tricerabutt.'

They all stared helplessly at the triple-cheeked beast as it lumbered towards them, picking up speed as it came.

Zack gulped.

In the space of a single morning they'd been giant-brown-blobbified, travelled millions of years into the past, been involved in a wild bum chase, travelled millions of years into the future and been attacked by not one but *two* tyrannosore-arses. They needed a tricerabutt attack like they needed a hole in the head . . . or *three* holes, as was a very real possibility in this situation.

'Gee,' said Zack. 'The Cretaceous is a really fun place. We should come here more often.'

'We'll be lucky to get out alive,' said Eleanor.

The tricerabutt snorted as it ran.

The stink made Zack feel faint.

The bum-fighters were in trouble.

Big trouble.

Bad trouble.

Triple trouble.

They didn't have time to run back to where they'd come from. The jungle was too dense. And running forward was out of the question.

Then Zack had an idea.

'Stand back, everyone,' he said.

'What are you going to do?' said Zack's bum, backing away with Ned and Eleanor.

Zack pulled what was left of his bum-fighter's certificate out of his bum-fighting belt and, using the two top corners, held it out to one side, matador-style.

'Be careful, Zack!' said his bum.

' "Careful" is my middle name,' said Zack.

'No, it's not,' said his bum. 'It's Henry!'

'Shut up!' said Zack.

Zack Henry Freeman took a deep breath and focused. 'You want a piece of me?' he said to the charging tricerabutt. 'Come and get it!'

CHAPTER 29

OLÉ!

The tricerabutt needed no encouragement.
It was already halfway across the clearing.

Zack had barely fluttered the sheet of paper in his hand and stepped nimbly to one side before the triple-cheeked brute charged past him, snorting great clouds of methane.

'Bravo!' yelled Zack's bum.

'Olé!' said Zack, feeling slightly dizzy from the double dose of noxious fumes issuing forth from between the tricerabutt's three cheeks.

The tricerabutt smashed uselessly into the undergrowth at the other end of the clearing. It pulled itself out, turned to face Zack and began charging once more.

'Olé, again!' said Zack, jumping out of the way at the last moment as the beast charged past him.

'Good going, Zack,' said Eleanor.

But Zack was not feeling well. He was desperately trying to fight the methane fog that was starting to cloud his thinking.

The tricerabutt turned once again and lowered its cheeks so that its three deadly warts were pointing directly at Zack.

It pawed the ground and began its run.

Zack tried to concentrate. With great difficulty. To his alarm he saw not one, but *three* separate tricerabutts coming at him. He waved his certificate first at one, then the other, and then at the third.

'Zack!' yelled his bum, who had figured out that Zack was suffering methane-induced triple vision. 'Close one eye!'

But, although this was excellent advice, Zack was too far gone to understand – or even to hear – what his bum was saying to him. He doubled over in a violent coughing fit.

'Zack!' yelled his bum. 'Get up! It's coming!'

But Zack was coughing too hard to hear his bum's warning. Or the thundering of the tricerabutt's hoofs.

Zack's bum ran to Zack and tried to pull him out of the way. But Zack, now on his knees, was too heavy for the small bum to move.

The tricerabutt, sensing a kill, lowered its mighty wart-horns close to the ground as it closed in on its helpless quarry.

'Leave me,' spluttered Zack. 'Save yourself while there's still time!'

'Not on your life!' said his bum, taking the certificate from Zack's hand. 'It's one for all and all for one! Got a match?'

CHAPTER 30

FIRE

Zack's bum jumped on top of Zack, pulled a match from his bum-fighting belt and lit one corner of the certificate.

'Hey!' protested Zack. 'That's my certificate!'

'It's mine, too!' said his bum, waving the certificate at the tricerabutt, which, despite its superior size and wart-horn power, screeched in terror at the sight of the naked flame.

The tricerabutt was running too fast to stop, however, and the best it could do was to swerve – a move which sent it sliding head-on towards the trunk of a particularly thick bumnut tree.

WHAM!

It hit the tree with such force that all three of its wart-horns lodged deep into the trunk.

Zack's bum screamed in pain and dropped the burning paper.

Zack quickly stamped on the flames and put what was left of the certificate back into his belt.

He looked at the tricerabutt. It was scraping the ground with its foot, snorting and desperately trying to pull its wart-horns out of the tree.

'Well done!' Zack said to his bum.

'Always happy to help,' said Zack's bum. 'Now, let's get out of here!'

'With pleasure,' said Zack, scooping up his bum and running to catch up with Eleanor and Ned, who were at the edge of the clearing, trying to find a way into the dense undergrowth.

'This is hopeless,' said Eleanor, pushing against a thick curtain of vines. 'There's no way in.'

'Psst!' said a voice a few metres away. 'In here!'

Eleanor looked at Zack. 'Did you say something?' she said.

'No,' said Zack. 'I thought you did.'

'It wasn't me,' said Eleanor, turning to Ned. 'Was it you?'

'Not me,' said Ned. 'I thought it was Zack's bum.'

'Nope,' said Zack's bum, pointing to a tangled thicket of bum creeper. 'It came from in there. Whoever – or whatever – it is, I think it wants us to go in.'

'Well, what are we waiting for?' said Eleanor. 'Anything's got to be better than staying here.'

'I don't know,' said Ned. 'Seems a bit risky.' But at that moment the tricerabutt succeeded in pulling its horns out of the tree-trunk. It turned on the helpless bum-fighters and, seeing they were without flame, began another charge. 'Then, again,' said Ned, 'maybe it's worth a shot.'

They hacked their way in.

Just in time.

Zack felt the tip of one of the tricerabutt's sharp warts brush his foot as he scrambled into the jungle's undergrowth behind the others.

CHAPTER 31

RESCUED

Z ack pushed his way through the undergrowth into an old hollow bumnut-tree log.

It was dark and wet and mushy. He could feel the moisture seeping through his clothes. But at least it was safe.

And it was definitely a lot better than being torn to pieces by tyrannosore-arses or skewered on the end of a tricerabutt's wart-horn.

As Zack's eyes adjusted to the darkness he saw a small bum, not unlike his own, standing in front of him. It looked as if it had been living rough. Its dirty skin was caked in mud, scratches and scars.

'You idiots!' the bum said. 'What were you doing out there? This is a dangerous place!'

'We know,' said Zack. 'But we didn't have much choice. Our craft was attacked by tyrannosore-arses. We had to make a run for it.'

'You have a craft?' said the bum, brightly. 'One that could take us out of here?'

'We *had* a craft,' said Eleanor. 'We're not sure if we still do. She wasn't doing too well, last time we saw her.'

'Oh,' said the bum, its cheeks sagging with obvious disappointment. 'Never mind. It's good to have your company at least. Even if you were stupid enough to come to this awful place.'

'We're not stupid,' said Zack's bum, eyeing the new bum suspiciously. 'And we're not idiots, either.'

'Then what are you doing here?' said the bum.

'What are *you* doing here? That's the question,' said Zack's bum.

'It wasn't my choice,' said the bum. 'I'll tell you that much! I was sucked into a brown hole.'

'You mean you're not a bumosaur?' said Zack's bum.

The small bum was taken aback. 'That's the kind of dumb question I'd expect from a *head*. Do I *look* like a bumosaur?' it demanded.

'Um, no, not really,' said Zack's bum. 'I suppose I just thought . . .'

'Well, you thought wrong,' said the bum. 'Bumosaurs are big, dumb and ugly. I, on the other hand, am small, smart and, even though I say so myself, quite cute.'

'And very argumentative,' said Zack's bum. 'Don't forget that.'

'You started it,' said the bum.

'No, I didn't,' said Zack's bum.

'You asked a stupid question,' said the bum.

'I didn't think it was *that* stupid,' said Zack's bum. 'And, besides, that's not the same as starting an argument.'

'As good as,' said the bum.

'No, it isn't!' said Zack's bum.

''Tis!' said the bum.

''Tisn't!' said Zack's bum.

'Stop it, both of you!' said Eleanor. 'We've got more important things to do than listen to your squabbling.' She turned to the small bum. 'Look,' she said. 'I don't know who you are or where you're from – we can deal with that later – but right now we are on a very important mission and you have to help us.'

'I've already helped you,' said the bum huffily. 'And I think I'm beginning to regret it.'

'Sorry,' said Eleanor. 'I'm a bit on edge. It's been a busy day.'

'You're telling me,' said the bum. 'I was woken first thing by an enormous explosion. I went to investigate, and would you believe it? It was a Great White Bumosaur! Just fell out of the sky!'

'You saw the Great White Bum?' said Zack.

'I saw *a* Great White Bumosaur,' said the bum.

'Was anybody else with it?' said Eleanor.

'Not that I saw,' said the bum. 'No "body", anyway. But there have been an awful lot of blowflies around this morning. Big ones, too. Disgusting things. Flying around vomiting over everything.'

'We've noticed,' said Eleanor. 'Where's the Great White Bumosaur now?'

The bum shrugged. 'I don't know. On its way to the Crack of Doom, I guess.'

'The Crack of Doom?' said Eleanor.

'Yes,' said the bum. 'It's where the Great White

Bumosaurs breed. I expect it will be looking for its own kind. It's no fun being alone, you know.'

As they talked they could hear the tricerabutt snuffling around, hunting for them. In the distance the tyrannosore-arses screeched and hooted. The drone of giant mutant zombie blowflies filled the late afternoon air.

'How far away is this Crack of Doom?' said Eleanor.

'It's about three hours north of here,' said the bum.

'Can you take us there?' said Eleanor.

'I could,' said the bum, 'but you don't want to go there.'

'Yes, we do,' said Zack's bum.

'No, you don't,' said the bum.

'Do!' said Zack's bum.

'Don't!' said the bum.

'Knock it off,' said Zack to his bum. 'You're not helping.'

'I didn't start it,' said Zack's bum.

'Yes, you did!' said the bum.

'No, I didn't!' said Zack's bum.

'Will you take us there or not?' said Eleanor loudly.

'You've got to be joking!' said the bum. 'It's un-believably dangerous. There are bumcanoes, giant stinkants, stinkbogs, chasms and every type of bumosaur you can imagine between here and the Crack of Doom.'

'How soon can we start?' said Eleanor. 'We're in a bit of a hurry.'

CHAPTER 32

DESPERATE

'**B**ut you don't seem to understand,' said the bum nervously. 'Not even the most desperate of fools would undertake such a dangerous journey with so little chance of success.'

'We *are* desperate,' said Zack. 'The Great White Bum is planning to send all the Great White Bumosaurs into the future, where they will completely destroy the Earth. We've already seen the results. Total destruction. Of everything. Bumageddon!'

'Bumageddon?' whispered the bum.

CHAPTER 33

BUMAGEDDON!!!

'Bumageddon,' said Eleanor, nodding.
    'Bumageddon,' said Ned.
    'Bumageddon,' said Zack's bum.
    'Bumageddon,' said Zack. 'And you are our only hope of stopping it.'
    The bum nodded solemnly. 'I understand,' it said. 'If that's the case, and you're sure that's where you need to go, then I'll be your guide. But you have to do exactly as I say, agreed?'
    The bum-fighters all nodded.
    All the bum-fighters, that is, except Zack's bum.
    Zack prodded it.
    'OK,' it mumbled reluctantly.

CHAPTER 34
SUSPICION

They set off with the small bum leading the way and Zack's bum bringing up the rear.

The harsh sounds – and horrible smells – of strange bumosaurs filled the air. As they walked, Zack used a large branch to swat away a giant mutant zombie blowfly that was circling his head.

'Hurry up,' said Zack to his bum. 'I don't want to get too far behind.'

'I *am* hurrying,' said his bum.

The giant mutant zombie blowfly swooped in again, almost knocking Zack over.

Zack poked it in the eye with the branch.

Hard.

So hard, in fact, that black jelly spurted out all over him. 'Gross!' said Zack, jumping backwards as the giant mutant zombie blowfly buzzed angrily and flew away.

Zack hated giant mutant zombie blowflies. Almost as much as he hated the Great White Bum.

'Zack!' whispered his bum.

'What is it?' said Zack, stopping to wipe large handfuls of the zombie blowfly's gooey eyeball slime off his clothes.

'Don't you think it's a little strange that a bum would choose to live out here all by itself?'

Zack – whose sense of what was strange had, in the past few months, undergone a similar expansion to his sense of what was dangerous – shrugged. 'But it didn't choose to live here,' he said, warily watching for the zombie blowfly's return. 'It was sucked into a brown hole.'

'So it says,' said his bum. 'But it could be lying. It could be leading us into some sort of trap. It could be working for the Great White Bumosaurs. We could be sacrifices!'

'Good theory,' said Zack. 'But you're forgetting one thing. We *asked* it to take us to the Crack of Doom. And it tried to talk us out of it.'

'I don't like it,' muttered Zack's bum. 'I don't like it at all . . .'

'Relax,' said Zack. 'It's harmless. And, you've got to admit, a bit cute.'

'Cute!?' said Zack's bum, flushing red. 'Are you kidding?'

'Are you blushing?' said Zack.

'As if,' said Zack's bum, flushing even redder.

'You *are* blushing!' said Zack. 'You know what I think?'

'No,' said Zack's bum, 'and I'm not interested.'

But Zack was on a roll. 'I think,' he said, 'I think you like . . .'

'ZACK!' yelled his bum. 'Watch out!'

CHAPTER 35

POOPASAUR

Zack froze before he could finish the sentence. Out of the corner of his eye he saw a dark shape lunging towards him. At first he thought it was the zombie blowfly returning, but then he noticed that it was the wrong colour.

It was brown.

With big teeth.

And bad breath.

And an even worse temper.

CHOMP!

The brown monster's jaws snapped down hard just a few millimetres short of Zack's nose. The stench of its breath brought tears to Zack's eyes. Before he could do anything, however, the brown monster reared back and lunged forward for another bite.

Zack stared.

It was ugly. *Really* ugly. It had two tiny black eyes and an enormous mouth. Its chunky brown skin was cracked like dried-out mud.

It struck again.

Zack threw himself, face first, on to the ground.

Again, the monster's teeth closed on air.

The others were too far ahead to be of any help.

'Well, don't just stand there!' Zack yelled at his terrified bum. 'Do something!'

'What?' said Zack's bum.

'Anything!' said Zack.

Zack's bum began to dance. 'You put your left hand in, you put your left hand out . . .' it sang.

'Anything *but* the hokey-cokey!' yelled Zack, as he watched the enormous brown serpent-like creature rearing back for a third attack.

Zack's bum picked up a stick and, using it as a cane, began a rudimentary tap dance.

'Not *that*, either!' said Zack.

'But I don't know any other dances!' said Zack's bum.

The monster hurled itself forward.

Zack, reeling under the withering blast of its breath, rolled over on to his back and prepared to kick it.

But there was nothing to kick.

It was all mouth.

Just as the brown monster was about to engulf Zack, however, their guide bum appeared.

It bent over, took aim and fired.

The monster's head snapped backwards. With a yelp it withdrew into the jungle as quickly and mysteriously as it had emerged.

Zack sat up, blinking. 'Thanks,' he said.

'Are you all right?' said the bum.

'I think so,' said Zack. 'What *was* that?'

'A poopasaur,' it said. 'There are a lot of them about this year.'

'A poopasaur?' said Zack.

' "Big, lumbering and deadly",' said Ned, reading from his book as he rushed towards them. ' "Lives in bumnut-tree forests. Prone to jumping out from undergrowth unexpectedly".'

'Well, lucky you brought that book, Ned,' said Zack, shaking his head. 'I never would have guessed otherwise.'

'Just trying to be helpful,' said Ned.

'Keep your eyes open, everybody,' announced their guide. 'This is a dangerous place.'

As they resumed walking, Zack's bum tapped Zack on the leg.

'That was no accident, Zack,' it said. 'It's trying to kill us.'

'How do you figure that out?' said Zack. 'That bum just saved me from a poopasaur. Which is more than I can say for you!'

Zack's bum reddened. 'Yeah, well, how come it didn't say anything about poopasaurs before?'

'It tried to convince us that it was too dangerous to go to the Crack of Doom in the first place,' said Zack.

'But it didn't warn us about poopasaurs!' said Zack's bum. 'Not specifically.'

'Well, no,' said Zack. 'But . . .'

'See what I mean?' said his bum. 'This is not a bum to be trusted.'

Zack shrugged. 'We don't have much choice,' he said.

CHAPTER 36

CAMPFIRE

That night the three bum-fighters and two bums sat around a small campfire. Long, low poopasaur mating calls filled the air.

Zack looked up into the blackness and marvelled at the awesome wash of stars above them. It was all so beautiful, he thought. It was hard to believe that a life-on-Earth-destroying arseteroid could come out of such a sky. But it was definitely coming. And soon.

Ned and Eleanor were roasting bumnuts the size of baseballs. 'These are much bigger than the bum-nuts back home,' said Ned, spitting out small pieces of the woody nut as he spoke.

'I know,' said their guide. 'Bumolution is not always for the better.'

'You can say that again,' said Zack's bum. 'Bums would have been so much better off without heads messing things up.'

Zack ignored his bum's remark and turned to their guide. 'So, how did you come to be here, exactly?'

said Zack. 'I know you got sucked into a brown hole, but what were you doing out in space to begin with?'

'Well,' said the bum, staring into the fire, 'it's a sad story. I used to have an owner. A really good one. She took care of me. Clothed me. Wiped me. Even let me watch television occasionally. She was the best owner a bum could ever want. But then one day I woke up and she wasn't there. I wasn't in her bed. I was in a rubbish bin. I'd been cut loose. Discarded. Abandoned.'

'Zack would never do that to *me*,' said Zack's bum. 'Would you, Zack?'

Zack raised his eyebrows. 'Wouldn't I?' he said.

Zack's bum ignored Zack. 'You must have done something pretty bad,' it said to the other bum.

'I never did anything!' said the bum. 'At first I thought there must have been some mistake – some terrible misunderstanding. Had I not done everything I could to be a good and faithful bum? Had I not fulfilled my half of the charter between a bum and its owner? I searched and searched for her but, alas, it was in vain. She had simply disappeared. Vanished.'

'That's too bad,' said Ned quietly.

Zack noticed that Eleanor was staring intently at the small bum through the smoke.

He supposed the bum's story couldn't have been easy for her to listen to. He knew how much she regretted her decision to cut her own bum loose all those years ago. Back then it had been a routine procedure for bum-fighters to replace their bums with false ones. No bum-fighter wanted to have their bum-fighting ability compromised by a bum that might not be completely loyal. But that was before she'd seen Zack and his bum in action – before she'd realised what a powerful team a bum and its owner could really be.

The small pink bum wiped a tear from its cheek.

'So, what did you do then?' Zack asked the bum gently.

'I kept looking,' it said. 'I wandered the solar system, searching for her. I would have kept searching, too, but I got sucked into the brown hole and deposited here, with no way of getting back. But to tell you the truth, I'm not sure I'd *want* to go back, even if I could. I can be lonely here just as well as there. Besides, I'm not sure I'd recognise my owner now, even if I did see her again. She was a little girl, then – she'd be quite grown up by now.'

The bum fell silent.

The fire glowed low.

Something screeched in the distance.

It was the saddest story that Zack had ever heard.

Ned and Eleanor were both wiping their eyes.

Even Zack's bum was choked up. 'Do you have a tissue, Zack?' it whispered.

'Yes,' said Zack, pulling a tissue from his pocket and handing it to his bum.

'I hope you find your owner some day,' said Zack.

The bum shrugged. 'Thanks,' it said. 'You're nice. You don't need a spare, do you?'

Zack's bum bristled. 'No, he's fine for the moment, thanks,' it said.

'You're lucky to have an owner like him,' said the bum.

'True,' said Zack's bum. 'But he's even luckier to have a bum like me.'

Zack glanced at Eleanor. She seemed even sadder than before.

'We'd better get some sleep,' said the bum. 'We have a lot of ground to cover tomorrow.'

'Sleep?' said Zack's bum. 'With tyrannosore-arses, tricerabutts, giant stinkants and poopasaurs out there . . . I'm not going to sleep a wink.'

'Good!' said their guide. 'Then you're on guard duty. Keep the fire burning and whatever you do, *don't fall asleep*. Understand?'

'There's not much chance of that,' said Zack's bum.

'What, not much chance of you understanding or not much chance of you falling asleep?' said their guide.

'Ha ha, very funny,' said Zack's bum. 'Good-night.'

Zack, Ned and Eleanor lay down on their bum-nut-leaf beds and were asleep within minutes.

Five minutes later the guide bum dozed off.

And, five minutes after that, so did Zack's bum.

CHAPTER 37

STINKANT-NAPPED

I t was dark when Zack awoke.
He blinked a few times and tried to remember
where he was. He had been so tired that he hardly
even remembered falling asleep. One moment he'd
been studying Eleanor's sad face across the smoke of
the campfire and the next moment . . . well . . . now
he was lying in pitch darkness.

He shut his eyes tightly and opened them again.

He'd had a dream, he remembered that much.

A crazy dream.

He'd dreamed that the fire had gone out and that
a gigantic red stinkant had picked him up in its pincers and carried him off to an underground stinkant
nest.

As Zack remembered his dream it seemed so vivid
that he could actually hear the scuttling and digging
noises the stinkants made.

And he could smell the dank earth of the underground nest and feel stinkant juice on his hands.

Where was the fire? he wondered.

As they'd been setting up camp the previous evening their guide bum had been at great pains to point out the importance of fire in protecting them from the night-time predators of the prehistoric world. But now the fire was completely out.

He looked up.

Before he'd gone to sleep there'd been a stunning canopy of stars above them.

Now there was nothing.

No fire.

No stars.

No sky.

What was going on?

Zack became aware of a pain around his waist. A dull, aching pain. The sort of pain that you might have felt if you'd been picked up by, say, a pair of giant stinkant pincers . . .

Oh no, thought Zack. 'Eleanor?' he said. 'Are you awake?'

'Zack?' said Eleanor groggily. 'What happened to the fire?'

'I'm afraid I've got some bad news,' said Zack.

'What now?' said Eleanor.

'I think we've been stinkant-napped,' said Zack. 'We may be in great danger.'

The scuttling sounds grew louder. Whatever was making them was definitely coming closer.

'Have you got a match?' said Zack.

'Yes,' said Eleanor. 'Hang on.'

Eleanor struck the match.

'Uh-oh,' said Eleanor as the tiny yellow glow

confirmed Zack's worst fears. 'I think you're right.'

Zack nodded as he looked around. They were in an underground chamber with rough-hewn rock walls. Just the two of them. His bum was missing.

So was Ned.

And so was their guide.

'How do we get out of here?' said Eleanor, striking another match.

'Same way we got in, I think,' said Zack.

'And how was that?' said Eleanor.

'I don't know,' said Zack. 'I was asleep. Sort of.'

'Ouch,' said Eleanor. The match she was holding had burned down to her fingertips. She pulled another from the box, struck it and peered into the darkness.

'What's that?' she said.

'What?' said Zack.

'On the wall over there – it looks like writing,' said Eleanor. 'I'm going to go and see what it says.'

'I'm coming with you,' said Zack, who was getting a little creeped out by the darkness and the scuttling sounds.

The two bum-fighters tripped and stumbled their way across the rocky floor to the far wall of the cave.

At the rock-face Eleanor lit a match and leaned in close.

They were words all right.

Words smeared on to the wall in a wet, glistening paste.

Zack began reading aloud: ' "WARNING! THE GREAT WHITE BUM IS . . ." '

His voice faltered as he recognised the words.

'That's the warning Ned saw!' said Eleanor. 'Only

these words aren't millions of years old. They're *fresh*!'

The match in Eleanor's hand went out.

'They might be fresh,' said Zack. 'But we're still too late.'

Suddenly Zack was blinded by a light shining directly into his eyes.

'You're not too late yet, soldier!' said a voice. 'But · you certainly took your time.'

Although Zack couldn't see a thing, he had no trouble identifying the voice.

'Gran!' he said. 'Is that you?'

CHAPTER 38

GRAN

'Of course it's me!' said Gran.
      'And me!' said the Forker.
'And me!' said the Flicker.
'But didn't you . . . don't you all . . . *die* here?'
said Zack, struggling with the complications of time
travel.
'First I've heard about it,' said Gran. 'Unless you
know something that I don't.'
Zack gulped . . . and quickly shook his head.
'Pincher,' said Eleanor, changing the subject, 'it's
great to see you, but can you turn that torch away –
it hurts!'
'Sorry,' said Gran, lowering her torch.
'Where are we?' said Zack.
'We're in a stinkant nest,' said Gran. 'Where do
you think? Ferocious little creatures. A lot bigger
than the ones back in my day. I mean, the ones *to
come* in my day . . . when I'm born, that is. Damn
this time travel! It does my head in!'

'Look, it's *simple*,' said the Forker. 'We've been over it and over it and over it! You were born in the future. Then you came back here to the past. But just because you are in the past doesn't mean that you *weren't* born in the future – it just means that you haven't been born in the future *yet* – not technically anyway – even though you *were* because how could you be here if you *weren't*? Understand?'

'No, I don't,' said Gran. 'How could I be born in the future?'

'You *weren't* born in the future!' said the Forker. 'For goodness' sake!'

'Language!' said Gran.

'"Goodness" is not a swear word!' said the Forker.

'No, but I don't like the tone of your voice,' said Gran. 'I'll thank you to remember your manners.'

'Sorry,' said the Forker. 'All I was trying to say was that you weren't born in the future.'

'But you told me I was,' said Gran.

'What he means,' said the Flicker helpfully, 'is that you *were* born in the future, but when you were born the future wasn't the future. It was the present. Not the *present* present, of course. The *future* present. But nevertheless, the present in which no past or future exists. Where the confusion comes in is that from where we stand at the moment *that* present is our future. Get it?'

'So I was born in . . . the present?' said Gran.

'Yes, the *future* present,' said the Flicker triumphantly. 'Which is now in *our* past, of course.'

'So I was born in our past future present,' said

Gran. 'Now I'm even more confused than ever!'

'It doesn't matter!' said Eleanor, impatiently.

'It may not matter to you, young lady,' said Gran, 'but my birth matters a great deal to me!'

'I'm sorry,' said Eleanor. 'Your birth matters a great deal to me, too, it's just that we're running out of time. When did you last see the Great White Bum?'

'We were spat out of the brown hole right behind him,' said Gran, 'straight into the middle of a crowd of giant mutant zombie blowflies. Luckily they concealed our arrival and we were able to hide. We heard him talking to himself – ranting and raving about how he was going to get revenge and send the Great White Bumosaurs back through the brown hole to Bumageddonise the future Earth. We tracked him as far as we could but then we got chased by an enormous hairy bum.'

'It was horrible,' said the Flicker. 'Took every towel I had to keep it at bay.'

'And every fork on my belt!' said the Forker.

'Yes,' nodded Gran. 'It gave us a run for our money. But by the time we'd got rid of it we'd lost the Great White Bum's trail.'

'We were trying to find the Great White Bum again when we were surrounded by stinkants,' said the Forker. 'They brought us here. We tried to escape but there were just too many of them. Then we had the idea of killing a stinkant and using its blood as paint to send you a warning about Bumageddon.'

'But how did you know we would see your message?' said Zack. 'It was deep underground in the Great Windy Desert. Ned Smelly only found it by sheer accident.'

'"Accident" is just another word for *fate*, Zack,'
said Gran, suddenly reminding Zack of a witch in
the dim gloom of the cave. 'Don't you remember
telling me what the Blind Bum-feeler foretold? She
said that you will free not just the world, but the
entire univarse from the scourge of bums past, present AND future!'

The words struck Zack like a triple lightning bolt.
'I know that's what she said,' said Zack slowly. 'But
what does "past, present and future" mean, exactly?'

'Oh that's easy,' said the Flicker. 'Let me
explain . . .'

'No!' said Eleanor. 'Not now. Something's coming. Play dead! And switch off the torch!'

CHAPTER 39

REUNITED

The bum-fighters dropped to the ground.

They could hear scuffling and shouting coming from the passage outside.

'Put me down!' yelled a shrill voice. 'Put me down!'

Zack smiled. 'That's my bum!' he said.

'Shhh!' hissed Eleanor.

'Wait until my owner finds out about this!' Zack's bum said. 'He'll tear this nest apart looking for me. And when he finds me he'll rip you to pieces!'

Zack heard a loud thud.

And then another.

'Ouch!' said his bum.

'Oof!' said a voice that Zack recognised as Ned's.

The bum-fighters listened as the scuttling receded back up the passage.

'You can run, but you can't hide!' yelled Zack's bum fiercely. 'You'll be sorry you ever messed with Zack Freeman's bum!'

'Steady on there,' said Ned. 'I hate to be a party

pooper, but a typical stinkant colony can consist of up to two hundred thousand stinkants and can have anywhere between ten thousand and twenty thousand food and egg chambers. Even if we *could* locate Zack and Eleanor – which is highly unlikely – it wouldn't be enough. It would take a small army of bum-fighters to fight our way out of here.'

'Which is exactly what we have, soldier!' said Gran, flicking her torch on.

'Mrs Freeman?' said Ned, picking himself up off the cave floor and throwing his arms around her. 'Am I glad to see you!'

'How are you, Ned?' she said. 'I haven't seen you since you were a boy. And now look at you!'

'Yeah,' said Ned. 'Come a long way, haven't I? Stuck in a stinkant nest in sixty-five million years BC.'

'Your mother would be proud,' said Gran. 'Meet the Flicker and the Forker!'

The bum-fighters shook hands.

'Pleased to meet you,' said the Flicker.

'We've heard a lot about you,' said the Forker.

'And I've heard a great deal about you!' said Ned. He noticed Eleanor and Zack. 'There you are! Good to see you both!'

'Zack!' said Zack's bum, jumping into Zack's arms.

'Where's our guide?' asked Eleanor.

'We don't know,' said Ned. 'Not with us. I take it it's not with you?'

'No,' said Eleanor. 'I hope it's all right.'

'Hmmph,' said Zack's bum. 'I'm *sure* it is.'

'What makes you say that?' said Eleanor, studying Zack's bum quizzically.

'Don't you get it?' said Zack's bum. 'It double-crossed us.'

'Double-crossed us?' said Eleanor. 'What do you mean?'

'It was obviously working for the stinkants all along. If I ever see that thing again I'll kill it!'

'That's highly unlikely,' said Ned. 'This place is like a maze. Took me two weeks to map the whole nest comprehensively. Even if you *did* know where it was, you'd be stinkant-meat long before you'd be able to locate it and kill it.'

'You've been here before?' said the Flicker.

'Yes,' said Ned. 'This is where I found your warning.'

'Do you still have the map?' said the Flicker hopefully.

'No,' said Ned. 'Not on me. It's in—'

'Shh!' said Eleanor. 'Listen!'

The scuttling in the passage outside the holding cave was getting louder.

And somewhere, far above them, they could hear the sound of muffled explosions.

CHAPTER 40

STOMP!

'Robobum!' said Ned, his eyes shining.

'We don't know that for sure,' said Eleanor.

'It's got to be!' said Ned.

'But even if it is Robobum, how will she find us?' said Zack. 'You said yourself there are at least ten thousand separate chambers.'

'Heat sensors,' said Ned.

'Yes, but how did she know we were in the stinkant nest in the first place?' said Zack's bum.

'That, I *don't* know,' said Ned, frowning.

The explosions were getting louder. Smoke and acrid fumes filled the air.

'Don't worry,' said Gran. 'We'll take care of it.'

'Yeah!' said the Flicker, cracking a rolled-up tea towel in front of him. 'This "Robobum" will regret the day it ever messed with me.'

'You mean *us*,' said the Forker, brandishing a large barbecue fork in his hand like a Japanese ninja sword.

'No,' said Ned. 'You don't understand! Robobum is our friend, not an enemy. I built her. She's a state-of-the-art bum-fighting machine in the shape of a Great White Bum!'

'Well, good for you, Ned!' said Gran. 'You always were a bit of a tinkerer.'

'A bum-fighting robot!' said the Flicker, letting his towel fall to his side. 'Now *that* I'd like to see!'

'Sounds like we soon will,' said the Forker, re-holstering his fork.

The scuttling sound of the stinkants was getting louder. Zack could feel the earth trembling all around them. Robobum was not so much navigating the passages of the nest as completely destroying them.

As the glare of daylight lit up the passage outside their cave, a river of stinkants surged past the opening. A lethal river of shiny red and black abdomens, thoraxes, legs and razor-sharp jaws. All rushing to attack Robobum.

The smell was horrible, and not helped by the fact that Robobum was incinerating her attackers as she made her way towards the cave holding the bum-fighters.

Huge hissing blasts of flaming insect repellent and thick acrid smoke filled the air. As Robobum came closer, the river of stinkants began to back up and then flow into the cave chamber.

'Everybody against the wall!' commanded Gran, as Robobum made a dramatic entrance.

The front line of stinkants reared back, snapping their jaws and squirting jets of foul-smelling juice at Robobum.

'Stand clear, please,' said Robobum in a calm and authoritative tone. 'Stand clear.'

But the stinkants did not stand clear. If anything, they redoubled their efforts.

'You were warned,' explained Robobum matter-of-factly. 'Have it your way!'

CHAPTER 41

ESCAPE?

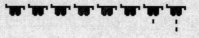

Z ack hoped Robobum wasn't about to blast the stinkants with a burst of flaming insect repellent.

She was too close.

Everyone in the chamber would be incinerated.

But Robobum had obviously already taken that into consideration.

Instead of using fire she simply started stamping.

The stinkants in the front line didn't stand a chance.

Robobum's powerful feet smashed through their tough armour, sending their putrid payloads of hot sticky stinkant juice splattering all over the chamber.

The stinkants pushed back further.

The bum-fighters were backed up against the wall – the Forker jabbing the ants with his fork and the Flicker flicking them with his rolled-up tea towel to prevent the frenzied mass from crushing them against the rock.

But Robobum kept stamping relentlessly until all

the stinkants in the chamber had been destroyed and all the stinkants outside the chamber were too scared – or too smart – to come in.

'Good work, Robobum!' said Ned. 'You're a hero!'

'Just doing the job I was programmed to do,' said Robobum.

'But how did you defeat those tyrannosore-arses?' said Eleanor. 'They looked like they were going to rip your fully riveted reinforced steel cheeks apart.'

'They did not know who they were dealing with,' said Robobum. 'I am Robobum. Fully riveted reinforced steel cheeks. Turbo-assisted jet-repulsion units. Nuclear wart-head equipped. Matter transport assisted entry and exit. Inside and outside voice options. Onboard tea- and coffee-making facilities. And I am self-wiping!!'

Eleanor nodded. 'Of course,' she said. 'Silly me. How could I have forgotten?'

'But how did you know we were in the stinkant nest?' said Ned.

'I was alerted to this fact by a cute pink bum,' said Robobum. 'It claims it was acting as your guide.'

'I knew it wouldn't abandon us!' said Eleanor, flashing an *I told you so* glance at Zack's bum. 'Where is it now?'

'It is inside my control centre,' said Robobum. 'I couldn't have found you without it. But enough talk. I advise immediate departure. Repeat. *Immediate* departure. Reinforcements are already on their way. Prepare for teleportation.'

As Robobum said this, she beamed her teleporting light down to where the bum-fighters were standing.

'Come on, Gran,' said Zack. 'Step into the light.'
'No, Zack,' said Gran, shaking her head sadly.

CHAPTER 42

GOODBYE

'**B**ut you're coming with us,' said Zack as he studied his gran's tired face. 'Aren't you?'

'No,' said Gran. 'At least, not yet. You see, we haven't finished our message to you. We'd run out of stinkant-blood paint, but with all these stinkant carcasses we've got enough to finish the job.'

'But it doesn't matter about the message any more!' said Zack. 'We've already seen it!'

'That's true,' said the Forker. 'But only because we're staying behind to finish it. If we don't finish it now, you won't be *able* to read it in the future, thus condemning the Earth to certain Bumageddon.'

'But . . .' said Zack.

'Don't worry about us,' said the Flicker. 'We can look after ourselves. We'll catch you up later.'

'No, you won't,' said Zack. 'If you stay you'll die here – all of you – we know because . . . because . . . *Ned saw your bones.*'

Gran put her hand on Zack's shoulder. 'We all have to die sometime,' she said.

'Yes, I know,' said Zack. 'But not *now*! First you, then my parents and now you . . . *again*! I'll be all alone.'

'Your parents?' said Gran, her fingers tightening on Zack's shoulder. 'James and Judi are dead? How?'

'They were squashed by a giant brown blob,' said Zack sadly. 'At the start of Bumageddon. *Everybody* was squashed – only a few of us made it out.'

Gran looked older and frailer as she absorbed the news. Then a change passed over her face – a look of cold determination. 'Then it's all the more important that we stay here and finish our task,' she said, hugging Zack. 'Goodbye, Zack. And good luck. The future of the world – and your parents – depends on you.'

'So, no pressure or anything,' said Zack's bum.

'Advise immediate departure,' said Robobum. 'I can sense reinforcements on the way. Prepare for immediate teleportation and departure.'

'Come on, Zack!' said Eleanor, leading him into the light. 'We have to go.'

Zack slowly let his gran go and stood in the teleportation beam with the others. Then, just before he dematerialised, he rushed back to Gran. He reached into his pocket and pulled out the cake of soap Ned had found in the cave. 'Here!' he said. 'This belongs to you.'

'Thanks, Zack,' said Gran. 'You're a good boy.'

Zack nodded, and resumed his place again under the light, tears in his eyes.

CHAPTER 43

QUESTIONS

As they rematerialised in the safety of Robobum's control room, they were greeted by their guide bum.

'You!' said Zack's bum.

'I'm very glad you're all right!' said Eleanor, rushing to its side.

'I'm very happy to see you all again,' it replied. 'I thought I might have been too late.'

Zack's bum eyed it suspiciously. 'How come you weren't stinkant-napped like the rest of us?' it said.

'I'm a very light sleeper,' said the bum. 'But even so, the stinkants were fast. By the time I realised what was happening it was all I could do to save myself.'

'Hmm, funny that,' said Zack's bum.

The bum shot Zack's bum an angry look. 'The real question,' it said, 'is how come *you* fell asleep and let the fire go out? You were on guard. It was your responsibility.'

'I just shut my eye for a second,' said Zack's bum, shuffling its feet. 'I was tired.'

'We all were,' said the bum. 'It's no excuse. You shouldn't have volunteered for guard duty if you weren't capable of staying awake.'

'I *didn't* volunteer for guard duty,' said Zack's bum. 'You *forced* me to do it.'

'I didn't force you to do anything!' said the bum. 'You could have said no.'

'I was too tired,' said Zack's bum. 'I didn't know what I was saying.'

'Never mind,' said Ned. 'What's done is done, and arguing about what *was* done won't undo it.' He turned to the guide. 'What I want to know is, how did you know about Robobum?'

'I *didn't*,' said the bum. 'Robobum found me. She was already looking for you. I just guided her here. All I really knew was that it would be the only way you could possibly be rescued from a stinkant nest.'

'I'm so proud of you!' said Eleanor. 'Well done!'

'Yes,' said Ned. 'Thank you.'

'Don't thank me,' said the bum. 'Thank Robobum.'

Zack's bum muttered something inaudible.

'I beg your pardon?' said the bum.

'Excuse me,' said Zack's bum, turning away and walking over to Zack.

Zack was standing in front of the screen watching his gran, the Forker and the Flicker resume their work on the wall as Robobum reversed out of the cave.

Eleanor came and stood beside him.

'We'll never see them again, will we?' said Zack.

'If I've learned anything in the last twenty-four

hours,' said Eleanor, 'it's never to say "never".'

'But why did they *all* have to stay?' said Zack.

'Because that's the way it happened,' said Eleanor. 'We can't change that. Besides, if your gran's soap wasn't there we would have thought Ned Smelly was just suffering methane madness. It all fits.'

'But we're trying to change the Great White Bum's evacuation plan,' said Zack.

'Some things we can change, others we can't,' said Eleanor. 'It's just the way it is.'

'Maybe we won't be able to change the evacuation plan, either,' said Zack.

'No,' said Eleanor. 'And then again, maybe we will.'

CHAPTER 44

CONFRONTATION

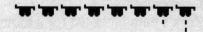

Robobum wasted no time extracting herself and her passengers from the stinkant nest.

Although the fighting was intense and at least another 30,000 unfortunate stinkants were stamped on or incinerated, Robobum eventually broke free, roaring up into the primeval dawn.

'Next stop, Crack of Doom,' she announced, taking off.

'No,' said Zack's bum. 'Next stop right now! We have a passenger to drop off.'

'What are you talking about?' said Zack. 'You can't get off!'

'Not *me*,' said his bum, pointing at their guide. 'It!'

'Me?' said their guide. 'What did I do?'

'It's what you *didn't* do that's the problem,' said Zack's bum. 'You didn't protect us from the stinkants!'

'I tried to!' said the guide. 'I put *you* on watch. It was *you* who fell asleep. If it's anyone's fault, it's *yours*.'

'It was all part of your evil plan!' said Zack's bum.

'What evil plan?' said Eleanor.

'Isn't it obvious?' said Zack's bum. 'It's working for the stinkants. It knew I wouldn't be able to stay awake. And while I slept it told them where to find us.'

'That's ridiculous,' said the guide. 'I came to save you, remember?'

Zack's bum hesitated for a moment, but it was on a roll and nothing could stop it.

'That was part of your evil plan, too,' said Zack's bum. 'You instructed the stinkants to capture us so you could save us so we wouldn't suspect that you put them up to it.'

'Listen to yourself!' said the guide. 'You're talking nonsense. Why would I be working for the stinkants? And even if I was, why would I care whether you knew it was me, once you were captured?'

'I don't know!' said Zack's bum. 'But that's exactly what I intend to find out!'

'You're crazy,' said the guide.

'And you're a dirty double-crossing stinkant-bum-kissing loser with no friends!'

The guide's cheeks flushed red with anger. 'You take that back!' it said.

'Make me!' said Zack's bum.

'With pleasure!' said the guide, launching itself at Zack's bum.

The two bums began scrapping on the floor – like wild dogs – in front of the stunned bum-fighters. It happened so fast that nobody had time to stop them.

Even Robobum was caught off guard. 'Bum-fight

on deck!' she announced, a little belatedly, as Zack's bum grabbed the guide in a double-handed cheek-lock and started to stretch it until it looked as if it would tear in two.

'I'll kill you!' said Zack's bum.

'Stop it!' yelled Eleanor, throwing a bucket of cold water on to the fighting bums.

The shock made Zack's bum lose its grip, and the two bums fell apart, panting heavily.

Zack immediately grabbed his bum's arm and twisted it up behind its back.

'Ow! Ow! Ow!' it yelled. 'Stop!'

'Only if you promise to stop fighting,' said Zack.

'OK,' said his bum. 'I'll stop . . .' Zack released his bum's arm. It immediately leaped at the guide and started fighting again. 'I'll stop when it's dead!'

'Zack! Control your bum!' said Eleanor, picking up the small pink bum and holding it above her head while Zack's bum jumped up and down underneath it, snapping angrily. 'Leave it alone, you maniac!' she said, booting Zack's bum in the left cheek.

'You stay out of this,' said Zack's bum. 'This is between us – it's got nothing to do with you!'

'That's where you're wrong,' said Eleanor. 'It's got everything to do with me.'

'Oh yes?' said Zack's bum. 'And why is that?'

'Because,' said Eleanor.

'Because why?' said Zack's bum.

'Because,' said Eleanor, 'it's *my bum*.'

CHAPTER 45

TRUTH

E leanor's words stopped the fight more effectively
than any number of buckets of cold water could
have.

'*Your* bum?' said Zack's bum.

'*Your* bum?' said Zack.

'*Your* bum?' said Ned.

'*Your* bum?' said Robobum.

'*Your* bum?' said Eleanor's bum.

'Yes,' said Eleanor. '*My* bum.'

CHAPTER 46

ABANDONED

'But ... but ... why didn't you say anything?' said Eleanor's bum. 'Didn't you recognise me?'

'I recognised you straight away,' said Eleanor. 'I wanted to say something, but I didn't know how to. Or how you'd feel about me. I thought you might be angry.'

'Angry?' said her bum, reddening. 'Who, me? *Angry*? Why should I be *angry*? I only tried to serve you as well as I knew how. I only tried to be there for you when you needed me. I only tried to be a good, solid, reliable, honest bum, and what did I get for my trouble? What did I get for my pain? What did I get for doing all the work that no other part of your body would – or could – do? I'll tell you what I got – chucked into a rubbish bin, without so much as a thank-you note! So why should I be angry? Of course I'm not angry. In fact, I don't think I can remember when I've ever felt quite so *not-angry*!'

'I'm sorry,' said Eleanor. 'But I didn't realise what

I was doing. When the Great White Bum killed my mother I knew I had to become a bum-fighter and that would mean having to get a false bum . . . I didn't know then what I know now: that bum-fighters and their bums can work together. That a bum can be a bum-fighter's best friend.'

'So that's all you want me back for,' said her bum. 'To make you a better bum-fighter. You just don't get it, do you?'

'No, that's not what I meant!' said Eleanor. 'I can understand how you feel, but . . .'

'No, you can't,' said her bum. 'You have no idea how it feels to be abandoned. But don't worry, you soon will.'

'What do you mean?' said Eleanor.

'Robobum!' said Eleanor's bum. 'Stop immediately! I'm getting off.'

'Affirmative,' said Robobum. 'Setting down now!'

'But you can't get off,' said Eleanor.

'And why not?' said Eleanor's bum.

'Because we'll never find the Crack of Doom without you!' said Eleanor.

'And?' said her bum.

'And what?' said Eleanor.

'And?' repeated her bum.

'And because you're my bum,' said Eleanor. 'I need you.'

'Right answer,' said her bum, 'just a little bit too late. Goodbye, Eleanor. I'm sorry it didn't work out between us.'

'Robobum has landed,' said Robobum. 'Safe to depart.'

'Teleport me out, please, Robobum,' said Eleanor's bum.

Eleanor watched sadly as her bum disappeared under the light.

'Good riddance, I say,' muttered Zack's bum quietly. But not quietly enough.

'Shut up!' snarled Eleanor. 'Or . . . or . . .'

'Or what?' said Zack's bum.

'Or *else*,' said Eleanor.

'Did you hear that, Zack?' said his bum. 'She threatened me.'

'*Shut up!*' said Zack.

CHAPTER 47

STUCK!

E leanor glared fiercely at Zack's bum. 'You're nothing but a troublemaker,' she said. 'How are we
supposed to find the Crack of Doom now?'

'Hey, don't blame me,' said Zack's bum. 'It's your
bum that's the troublemaker.'

'How dare you!' said Eleanor. '*You're* the one who
fell asleep on your watch. And if my memory serves
me correctly, wasn't it *you* who ran away in the first
place to help the Great White Bum build his bumcano? And you have the nerve to call *my* bum a
troublemaker?'

'Easy, Eleanor,' said Zack. 'That's all in the past
now.'

'And in case you hadn't noticed, chucklehead,'
said Eleanor, 'so are we! We're stuck here without
a map and now, thanks to your bum, no guide
either!'

'Negative,' said Robobum. 'That is not correct.
I can act as your guide.'

'But you've never been here before,' said Eleanor. 'You might have a BPS*, but there are no satellites here – they haven't been invented yet. So as far as I can figure, you're as lost as the rest of us.'

'Negative,' said Robobum. 'Although my BPS is currently not functioning, I am equipped with many other features. Let me remind you that I am Robobum. Fully riveted reinforced steel cheeks. Turbo-assisted jet-repulsion units. Nuclear wart-head equipped—'

'Spare us the details,' interrupted Eleanor.

'As you please,' said Robobum, undaunted by Eleanor's abruptness. 'My sensors indicate an abnormal concentration of methane in the mountainous region to our north-east. I believe this is where the Crack of Doom will be found.'

'How can you be sure?' said Ned. 'With all these prehistoric bums running around, wouldn't there be an abnormal concentration of methane over the entire planet?'

'The molecular signature of this particular methane is almost identical to that emitted by the Great White Bum,' said Robobum. I believe there is a ninety-five per cent probability of it belonging to a large number of the same types of Great White Bum. Furthermore and interestingly, it almost exactly corresponds with coordinates of where the arseteroid that pretty much wiped out life on Earth hit.'

'All right, then,' said Zack. 'What are we waiting for?'

Eleanor shrugged.

* **Bum positioning system. See Glossary.**

Ned nodded. 'Proceed to the Crack of Doom, Robobum,' he said.

'Affirmative!' said Robobum, roaring into action. 'Prepare for lift-off.'

Zack grabbed a handrail as Robobum rose into the air. But as fast as she had risen, Robobum returned to the ground.

'What's the matter, Robobum?' said Ned.

'Sorry,' said Robobum. 'I seem to be experiencing some difficulty. Prepare for relaunch.'

Robobum rose into the air again, higher this time, but only for a few seconds, before crashing to the ground once more.

'Lift-off status report!' said Ned.

'My undercarriage appears to be stuck,' said Robobum.

'Full thrust!' said Ned. 'Give it everything you've got.'

'Affirmative!' said Robobum, drawing on every bit of her nuclear stinkant-juice-powered twin-injected nitro-assisted engine's power.

Zack and Eleanor both put their fingers in their ears to block out the deafening roar.

But still Robobum remained earth-bound.

'Negative,' said Robobum. 'Robobum is immobilised. Recommend extra-vehicular excursion to establish and remove cause.'

'I'll go,' volunteered Zack.

'Good on you, Zack,' said his bum, jumping up and slapping him on the back. 'I knew we could count on you.'

'You're coming with me, you know,' said Zack.

'I'm not going out there without back-up. It's dangerous.'

'That's exactly why I'd prefer to remain here,' said his bum. 'Why don't you take Eleanor? She'll be more use to you.'

'Don't push your luck,' said Eleanor with quiet menace.

Zack's bum saw the look in her eyes. 'When do we leave?' it said.

'Right now,' said Zack.

CHAPTER 48

VINES

'Wow!' said Zack as he and his bum material-ised on to the ground in front of Robobum. 'Would you look at that!'

Robobum was perched on the edge of a deep canyon.

'That's some crack,' said his bum admiringly.

'It's so deep!' said Zack, trying to see the bottom.

'It's so wide!' said his bum.

Zack stared down into it for so long that he began to feel light-headed. He had to force himself to stop looking and concentrate on the job in hand.

It wasn't too hard to see why Robobum was unable to lift off.

She was caught in a messy tangle of pale grey vines. The vines were attached to a clump of trees and rocks and stretched right across the canyon like a giant spider web, except that the strands were as thick as rope.

'This stuff is everywhere,' said Zack's bum. 'What do you think it is?'

132

'Looks like some sort of vine or creeper,' said Zack, taking a piece in his hand. 'Pretty strong. And sticky, too. No wonder Robobum couldn't break free.'

Zack took his Bum-fighters' Army pocket knife out of his utility belt and began cutting.

It was hard work.

The vines were tough. They were made up of millions of strands wound tightly around each other to form a powerful bond.

As Zack cut slowly through the first vine – practically strand by strand – he was grateful for the stinkant juice, which had left a greasy coating on his hands. It allowed him to handle the vines without getting stuck to them.

He was halfway through cutting a second vine when he heard a voice.

It was a long way away, but definitely a voice.

'Can you hear that?' said Zack.

'Yes,' said his bum. 'And I can see where it's coming from, too.'

It pointed to the middle of the canyon.

Zack squinted.

There was something moving on the vines.

'Do you think it's Eleanor's bum?' said Zack.

'No,' said Zack's bum. 'It's not the right colour. And it's too big.'

'Do you think it's in trouble?' said Zack.

'It sounds like it,' said Zack's bum.

'Do you think we should help it?' said Zack.

'Definitely not,' said Zack's bum. 'It's totally off-mission. I think we should just cut Robobum free and get out of here.'

'But,' said Zack, 'we can't just leave it there!'

'Yes we can,' said Zack's bum, hacking into the vine. 'This is a dangerous place. If we get distracted, we die.'

They heard the strange gurgling cry again.

Zack looked at his bum. 'What if it was you out there?' he said.

'But it's not me,' said his bum.

'I know that,' said Zack. 'But *what if it was*? You'd want to be rescued, wouldn't you?'

'Y-yes . . .' said his bum. 'But . . .'

'Then that settles it,' said Zack. 'We're going.'

CHAPTER 49

BUMANTULA

Five minutes later Zack was crawling across the sticky vines towards the struggling figure, his bum perched on his shoulder.

'Aargh,' said his bum, looking down into the canyon. 'I'd hate to fall.'

'That makes two of us,' said Zack.

'It's *such* a long way down,' said his bum.

'Yes,' said Zack, gripping the vine tightly.

'You'd end up totally splattered,' said his bum. 'Splattered just like a rotten watermelon dropped from a . . .'

'Would you shut up!' said Zack, grimacing. 'You're not helping!'

Zack was all too well aware of how high they were.

And how far down they could fall.

But he was doing his best not to think about it. He was just climbing slowly – and very carefully – across the vines towards the moaning figure.

'What's it saying?' said Zack's bum as they crawled closer.

'I don't know,' said Zack. 'I don't know what language it's speaking. I don't even know what it is.'

It didn't seem to resemble anything he'd ever seen before – man, beast or bum – but, whatever it was, it was definitely trying to communicate with them.

It appeared to be made of flesh. Flesh that had been pulverised and mashed and then moulded into the rough shape of a man.

And it stank.

Bad.

Really bad.

Although he was no stranger to bad smells, Zack gagged as they came closer to the horrible creature. It appeared to be trying to form words, but was having great trouble doing so because its mouth was so crudely formed – like a hole in a piece of dough.

'Can you make out what it's saying now?' said Zack's bum.

'Something about great danger, I think,' said Zack.

'Um, Zack . . .' said his bum, the blood rushing from its cheeks, leaving it white and trembling and – for once – speechless.

'What's the matter?' said Zack. 'Are you all right?'

His bum just pointed to the far side of the canyon.

An enormous black shape was moving across the vines towards them.

An enormous black shape with two bulbous domes and eight legs.

Zack didn't have Ned's *What Bumosaur is That?* guide, but he didn't need it. He could see that it was a bumantula.

A *giant prehistoric* bumantula.

And suddenly – all too late – he could understand what the smelly creature meant by 'great danger'.

One thing was for sure. There was no time to save the creature. It was every man – or in its case, every *mutant* – for himself.

Zack turned around, but the hideous creature grabbed his leg. 'Don't leave me here,' it begged. 'Help me, Zack. Help me like I helped you!'

Zack froze.

The mutant knew his name!

CHAPTER 50

MUTANT

Zack stared at the mutant.

He looked into its eyes – two deep, bloodshot pools of pain – and recognised their owner.

It was the Mutant Zombie Maggot Lord. Or, to be more accurate, thought Zack, what *used* to be the Mutant Zombie Maggot Lord. The mass of putrefying flesh in front of him bore little resemblance to anyone – or anything – but Zack knew those eyes.

He'd known them when they'd belonged to the Kisser – the dirty double-crossing traitor to the bum-fighting cause. And, even after the Kisser had become the hideously deformed Mutant Maggot Lord – as a result of falling into a brown lake full of mutant maggots – Zack had still recognised his eyes. And Zack had looked into those eyes, for what he'd been sure was the final time, when the Mutant Zombie Maggot Lord had heroically sacrificed himself to his beloved, and by then zombified, maggots in order to allow Zack, his bum, Eleanor and the famous bum-fighting team of Mabel's

Angels to escape to freedom from the zombified Maggotorium. But what was he doing here? How was it possible that he was still alive? What had happened to this man . . . this beast . . . this . . . *mutant*?

'Zack!' yelled his bum, recovering its voice. 'Do something!'

Zack looked up.

The bumantula was closing in fast.

Its twin cheeks wobbled sickeningly as it picked its way across its web. And its shiny black fangs glistened.

Zack reached out to the Mutant Zombie Maggot Lord and grabbed the arm that he was holding out to him. Zack pulled as hard as he could.

'Aaaggghhh!' yelled the Mutant Zombie Maggot Lord.

Zack gasped.

He'd ripped the Mutant Zombie Maggot Lord's arm completely off his body.

'Careful!' yelled the Mutant Zombie Maggot Lord. 'I'm still very frail, you know.'

'What on earth happened to you?' said Zack, staring disbelievingly at the dripping arm and then at the Mutant Zombie Maggot Lord.

'Now is hardly the time,' said the Mutant Zombie Maggot Lord, 'but, as you know, I was eaten by mutant zombie maggots who then became mutant zombie blowflies. It seems they got sucked into the brown hole when chasing the Great White Bum's aroma as it escaped into space. What you don't know is that they vomited me back up when they got here.

I managed to pull the pieces of myself together again – or what was left of them – and then I got stuck in this stupid web.'

'That's awful,' said Zack, finding it impossible not to feel compassion for the former traitor. Not even a traitor deserved to be turned into a pile of zombie-blowfly spew.

'Yes,' said Zack's bum. 'Awful and *totally gross*.'

A look of pain passed over what remained of the Mutant Zombie Maggot Lord's face.

'Sorry,' said Zack. 'My bum can be very rude. It doesn't mean it.'

'Yes I do!' said his bum.

'Don't worry about it,' said the Mutant Zombie Maggot Lord, pointing. 'Worry about that!'

Zack turned around.

The bumantula was close.

Too close.

CHAPTER 51
ORIGAMI

The bumantula extended an enormous black leg towards Zack's heart. The lethal black tip shone like a spear.

Zack hit it with the only weapon he had available – the Mutant Zombie Maggot Lord's freshly amputated arm.

But it had no effect. He might as well have hit the bumantula with a stockingful of warm jelly. The arm splattered against the spider's leg and splashed all over Zack, his bum and the Mutant Zombie Maggot Lord.

'Hey!' said the Mutant Zombie Maggot Lord. 'That's my arm.'

'That *was* your arm,' said Zack's bum, wiping it off itself.

'Sorry,' said Zack.

'Good one, Zack!' said his bum.

'OK, Mr Smarty Pants,' said Zack. 'I'd like to see you do better.'

The tip of the spider's leg was only millmetres away from Zack's chest.

'All right, I will!' said Zack's bum. 'Watch this!'

Zack gasped as he watched his bum leap from his shoulder on to the bumantula's leg and use it as a bridge to get right up close to its glistening black fangs. 'Merry Christmas!' said Zack's bum, bending over and giving the bumantula a present it would never forget.

It had an instant effect. The huge beast withdrew its legs and contracted into a tight black ball as it tried to protect itself against the disgusting fumes.

'Phew,' said Zack, blocking his nose. 'What *have* you been eating?'

'You tell me!' said Zack's bum, leaping back on to his shoulder. 'I'm just the delivery boy. Let's get out of here!'

'Good idea,' said Zack, seizing the Mutant Zombie Maggot Lord's other arm – more gently this time. He pulled him free of the web and began climbing as quickly as he could back towards Robobum.

He could see, with a mixture of surprise and relief, that Eleanor and Ned were outside the ship, busy finishing the job of cutting Robobum's legs free of the web.

'Hurry, Zack!' said his bum. 'It's woken up!'

Zack, heart pounding, glanced behind him.

The bumantula, apparently recovered from its gassing and far more agile on the web, was bearing down on them. Fast.

It wasn't helping that Zack was burdened with the combined weight of his bum and the Mutant Zombie Maggot Lord.

Zack looked up and saw the bumantula's fangs, like twin black tusks of death, bared and dripping with venom.

And then Zack did a strange thing.

He stopped, took what remained of his bumfighter's certificate out of his utility belt and began folding it.

'Are you out of your tiny bum-fighting mind, Zack?' yelled his bum. 'Now is definitely not the time for origami.'

'It's not origami,' said Zack, smoothing it out and holding it up for his bum to see. 'It's a paper plane. See?'

'Great, Zack,' said his bum in disbelief. 'Well, it was nice knowing you. Right up to the point where you got methane madness.'

'I don't have methane madness,' said Zack. 'Watch!'

Zack launched the paper plane. It flew, straight and true, right into one of the bumantula's eight brown eyes.

Once more it contracted in pain, giving Zack the crucial break he needed to reach the edge of the canyon, disentangle himself from the web and run towards Robobum.

Eleanor and Ned were just finishing cutting through the remaining strands of the web as Zack rushed up.

'Hey, that was my job,' said Zack, panting.

'You're telling me!' said Eleanor. 'What were you thinking? You had one simple task and you decide to go bumantula hunting instead! What's the matter with you? And what's that?' Eleanor was pointing with one hand at the pile of putrid flesh cradled in Zack's arms, and blocking her nose with the other.

'An old friend,' said Zack.

CHAPTER 52

TRAPPED!

'Clear!' said Ned, cutting through the last strand of web. 'Everybody back inside!'

As they assembled underneath Robobum, the bumantula was just reaching the edge of the canyon.

On the web it had moved fast, but on the ground it moved even faster.

'Teleport us up, Robobum!' said Ned, staring at the rapidly advancing bumantula. 'On the double!'

Zack felt Eleanor's hand clutch his arm tightly as the bumantula leaped at the huddled bum-fighters.

They dematerialised just in time.

Back inside Robobum, Ned wasted no time. 'Lift-off!' he commanded.

Robobum, anticipating Ned's command, was already rising into the air.

'You can let go,' said Zack to Eleanor, who was still holding his arm. 'We're safe now.'

'Oh, yes, of course,' said Eleanor, quickly releasing her grip. 'Sorry . . .' she said.

'It's OK,' said Zack.

'No, it's *not* OK,' said Eleanor, getting to her feet. 'None of this is *OK*.'

Suddenly Robobum listed steeply to one side.

Eleanor and Ned staggered backwards.

Zack looked at the screen. But it was dark. 'What's happening?' said Zack.

'Bumantula clinging to Robobum's exterior,' announced Robobum.

'Full thrust!' commanded Ned.

Robobum applied full thrust.

Despite the bumantula's deadly embrace, Robobum continued to rise into the sky, although more slowly and unsteadily than before.

'Can't you get rid of it?' said Eleanor.

'I am doing my best,' said Robobum. 'But this contingency was not programmed into my system.'

'I would have thought that was true for pretty much everything on this whole mission!' said Eleanor.

'You're right,' said Ned, 'but our best bet is to keep rising. When we get to a high enough altitude, the bumantula will simply freeze to death.'

'If we don't get crushed to death on the way,' said Zack's bum.

Ned shrugged. 'Don't worry. Robobum's outer shell is made of double-strength steel. She survived a twin tyrannosore-arse attack. I don't think a bumantula – even one this big – is going to pose too much of a threat.'

'Oh yeah?' said Eleanor. 'Then how do you explain that?'

There was a loud groaning noise. The walls of the

control room were starting to warp and buckle.

'Bumantula crushing Robobum,' announced Robobum matter-of-factly. 'Robobum losing altitude.'

Zack could feel his stomach somewhere up around his throat.

Eleanor was right.

Things were not OK.

In fact, things could hardly get much worse.

They were dropping.

Fast.

And the walls were closing in.

CHAPTER 53

CRUSH!

Robobum hit the ground with a sickening crunch. Zack was thrown to the floor.

He looked up at the ceiling.

There were two large bulges. And they were getting bigger.

Zack screamed.

It could only mean one thing.

Or, rather, *two* things.

The bumantula's fangs!

Zack's mouth went dry.

If those fangs broke through, the amount of venom that would be released into the cabin would be nothing less than torrential.

And if they weren't drowned in the bumantula's venom they could look forward to being crushed to death by its powerful legs.

And if they were really lucky, Zack decided, maybe both would happen at the same time.

At least they wouldn't suffer much, he thought.

But that was small consolation. The hardest part was waiting.

'Warning! Warning!' announced Robobum. 'Bumantula biting and crushing Robobum. Repeat. Bumantula biting and crushing Robobum!'

'Yeah, I think we get the picture, thanks,' said Ned gloomily as his greatest creation crumbled around him.

'Warning! Warning!' said Robobum.

'We *know*!' said Ned.

'No,' said Robobum. 'A *new* warning. Great White Bum approaching!'

'Wonderful!' said Eleanor. 'This day just keeps getting better and better.'

Zack gulped. Eleanor's sarcasm was the last thing he – or anyone else – needed. Rivets were popping and falling around them. The fang points in the ceiling were becoming more and more clearly defined. Robobum was helpless against the bumantula and now the Great White Bum was here to finish them off.

The noise of buckling metal was deafening.

Zack braced himself.

His bum braced itself.

Eleanor braced herself.

Ned braced himself.

The Mutant Zombie Maggot Lord tried his best to brace what little self there was left of him to brace.

And then . . .

CHAPTER 54
NOTHING

. . . nothing.

CHAPTER 55

GIFT

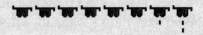

Well, nothing *bad*, at least.

The noise stopped.

The bum-fighters opened their eyes. They held their breaths.

The roof stopped bulging.

Nobody dared to exhale in case the nightmare began again.

But it didn't.

In fact things got even better.

The bumantula's legs released their grip on the outside of Robobum and disappeared, revealing a sight so extraordinary and so unexpected that the bum-fighters wondered if they were suffering a collective delusion brought on by methane madness.

The Great White Bum was rescuing them!

He had prised the bumantula's powerful legs off Robobum and was now pulverising and pummelling the hapless bumantula into the ground.

'Great White Bum destroying bumantula,' reported

Robobum, quickly recovering from the near-fatal embrace.

'He will be destroying us next if we don't get out of here fast,' said Eleanor. 'Let's go!'

'But the Great White Bum is my friend,' said Robobum. 'He saved me!'

'He is not your friend,' spat Eleanor. 'Or anybody else's friend. He is the most evil bum in history!'

'Who you didn't want to kill when you had the chance,' said Zack.

'Who you *couldn't* kill when you had the chance,' said Eleanor.

'Who at least I *tried* to kill when I had the chance,' said Zack.

'Can you still fly, Robobum?' said Eleanor.

'I do not know,' said Robobum. 'I am creating a damage report now.'

'Oh, gross,' said Zack's bum. 'Look at that!'

Out of the window they could see that the Great White Bum was pulling the bumantula's legs off, one by one.

'He is such a bully!' said Zack's bum.

'Poor thing,' said the Mutant Zombie Maggot Lord. 'I can sympathise. I know how much that hurts.'

Eleanor rounded on him. In all the excitement she'd forgotten about him being there. 'Who – *and what* – are you, anyway?' she said.

'Ah, have you forgotten me so soon?' said the Mutant Zombie Maggot Lord. 'I, who sacrificed my life, so that you could live?'

Eleanor stared at him with wide eyes. 'Kisser?' she said. 'Is that you?'

'I *used* to be the Kisser,' said the Mutant Zombie Maggot Lord. 'But that was another lifetime ago. A couple, in fact. I'm somebody else now.'

'It's the Mutant Zombie Maggot Lord,' said Zack.

Eleanor regarded him with a mixture of suspicion, pity and disgust. 'But I thought you were eaten by the mutant zombie maggots!' she said.

'I was,' said the Mutant Zombie Maggot Lord. 'It was a *very* unpleasant experience.'

'But shouldn't you be dead?' said Eleanor, frowning.

'I was close enough to it,' said the Mutant Zombie Maggot Lord. 'For a little while, at least. But then the mutant zombie maggots turned into mutant zombie blowflies and I reconstituted myself from their spew.'

'You just don't give up, do you?' said Eleanor. 'I suppose we should really call you the Mutant Zombie Blowfly Spew Lord.'

'The *Mutant* Mutant Zombie Blowfly Spew Lord, to be completely accurate,' said Ned coldly. 'But we'll just call you "the Mutant Spew Lord" to keep things simple.'

'I expect that you're still angry about when I tried to kill you, back in the Great Windy Desert,' said the Mutant Spew Lord. 'But I really am sorry.'

'Angry?' said Ned. 'Me? Angry?' He was silent as he searched unsuccessfully for words to express exactly how angry he was. 'Apology *not* accepted!' he finally blurted before turning away.

'I understand,' said the Mutant Spew Lord. 'But I really have changed. Honestly! I was confused, back then. But now I'm on your side. I want to help you.'

'Oh, gross!' said Zack's bum. 'I think I'm going to be sick.'

'That's no way to speak to a guest,' said Zack. 'Even if he *is* going to make you sick.'

'I'm not talking about the Mutant Spew Lord,' said Zack's bum, pointing to the screen.

Zack looked up.

And gasped.

The Great White Bum was approaching Robobum with the still-quivering bumantula abdomen in his arms.

'Oh no!' said Eleanor. 'He's coming! Lift-off, Robobum!'

'Damage report not yet complete,' said Robobum.

'You'll have a lot more damage to report if you don't take off now!' said Eleanor. 'We'll be smashed to pieces!'

'I don't think so,' said Ned.

'What do you mean, you don't *think* so?' said Eleanor. 'You saw what he just did to the bumantula.'

'Look closely,' said Ned. 'The Great White Bum appears to be offering the bumantula cheeks to Robobum. If I didn't know better, I'd say . . .'

He hesitated.

'What?' said Zack, not daring to take his eyes off the Great White Bum, who was kneeling in front of them, holding the legless bumantula in his outstretched hands.

'Well,' said Ned, 'it sounds crazy, but if I didn't know better, I'd say the Great White Bum is offering Robobum a gift.'

CHAPTER 56

PROPOSAL

The bum-fighters stared at the Great White Bum. They weren't used to seeing him behaving so politely.

'But *why*?' said Eleanor. 'Why is he giving Robobum a present?'

'Robobum *is* a very good-looking bum,' said Ned, 'even if I do say so myself.'

'You mean,' said Eleanor, dumbfounded, 'the Great White Bum doesn't realise Robobum is just a machine? He thinks she's real?'

'Apparently so,' said Ned.

'We thought she was real at first, too, don't forget,' said Zack.

'Yes, but we're humans,' said Eleanor, 'not bums.'

'Speak for yourself,' said Zack's bum. '*I* thought she was real.'

Eleanor shot it a dangerous look. 'I'm still not speaking to you. Not now. Not ever.'

Before Zack's bum could respond, Robobum

interrupted. 'Request permission to accept gift from Great White Bum.'

'Permission granted,' said Ned, clearly pleased that his robotic bum was so convincing that she had fooled the Great White Bum himself. 'It wouldn't do to offend our new best friend, now, would it?'

Robobum stretched out her arms and received the pulsating prize in her hands. 'Thank you.'

'It is my pleasure to serve you,' rumbled the Great White Bum, his voice – but thankfully not the *smell* of his voice – being broadcast via the external microphone located in one of Robobum's fake pimples. 'This bumantula will not bother you again, and its juices make a very fine perfume, which will only enhance your loveliness.'

'Wow,' said Eleanor. 'What a charmer! Who would have guessed?'

The Mutant Spew Lord drew in his breath to speak, but was cut short by Ned.

'Shush!' said Ned. 'We can't afford for the Great White Bum to get suspicious.'

'But he can't hear us, can he?' said Zack.

'He shouldn't be able to,' said Ned, 'but after what Robobum's been through, we'd better be careful. There may be some gaps where sound can get through. Robobum, use your inside voice on the lowest possible setting.'

'Affirmative,' whispered Robobum.

'I trust the bumantula did not cause you too much distress,' said the Great White Bum.

Robobum considered the Great White Bum's enquiry. 'Negative,' she said, switching back to her outside voice. 'Damage report indicates minor malfunctions in control and navigation systems and moderate buckling of left outer cheek, but otherwise I am ninety per cent operational.'

Ned winced. 'Too much Robospeak,' he whispered to Robobum. 'Switch to casual mode.'

'Affirmative,' whispered Robobum. 'Oops, I mean, "OK"!'

But the Great White Bum didn't seem to notice or worry about Robobum's lapse. 'Why are you not at the Crack of Doom with the others?' he said. 'We are leaving very soon!'

'What should I say?' whispered Robobum internally.

'Ask for more information!' said Ned.

'Leaving?' said Robobum. 'Where to?'

'You weren't at last night's meeting, were you?' said the Great White Bum. 'I'm sure I would remember seeing a bum as lovely as you.'

'No,' said Robobum. 'I was on my way but I got stuck in the bumantula's web.'

'Of course,' said the Great White Bum. 'Forgive me, but there is so much to do. The Earth will soon be struck by a devarsetating arseteroid. It will wipe out all bumosaur life on Earth. Look into the sky. You can already see the glow.'

Robobum looked up, giving the bum-fighters a clear view of a tiny but bright point of light in the sky.

'Oh my goodness,' said Robobum. 'That's terrible!'

'Yes,' said the Great White Bum. 'But don't worry.

I have a plan for the complete evacuation of all Great White Bumosaurs from the planet.'

'That's what *you* think,' said Zack.

'Shush!' said the Mutant Spew Lord. 'We can't afford to miss anything!'

'In less than two hours every Great White Bumosaur on Earth will travel to the arseteroid-free future by means of a brown-hole time gate,' continued the Great White Bum. 'Once there, we will create a new world. A world of Great White Bums. I shall be their King, naturally. But what is a King without his Queen? I have travelled across time and space and have never met a Great White Bum as great or as white or as beautiful as you. What do you say? Will you consent to be my bride, my wife and my Queen, to rule alongside me over the greatest Great White Bum empire the univarse has ever known?'

The bum-fighters were gobsmacked.

They'd all learned to expect the unexpected from the Great White Bum, but none of them had expected this.

The Great White Bum was in love.

With Robobum!

CHAPTER 57
STALLING

The bum-fighters had known about the Great White Bum's plan for evacuation, of course, but they hadn't imagined in their wildest dreams that he would fall in love with Robobum. And judging by Robobum's silence, it was clear that neither had she.

'The Great White Bum's request falls outside mission protocols,' Robobum finally said to Ned. 'Request suggestion for appropriate response.'

'Tell him you need some time to think,' said Ned.

'Time to think about what?!' said Eleanor. 'Are you out of your mind? Robobum can't get married. Especially not to the Great White Bum!'

'Calm down, Eleanor,' said Zack. 'This might be just the break we need.'

'Zack could be right,' said Ned. 'It can't hurt to think this through properly. Go ahead, Robobum.'

'Thank you, Great White Bum, for your kind offer,' said Robobum. 'I am honoured, and flattered, of course. But it is such a big decision to make so quickly. Do you mind if I have a few moments alone to think about it?'

'What is there to think about?' said the Great White Bum. 'You won't find a bum greater or whiter than me! And certainly not in the time remaining on this planet.'

'I know,' said Robobum. 'But it's all very sudden, and I'd just like to be sure, that's all.'

'I understand,' said the Great White Bum. 'But we don't have much time. I shall return in five minutes for your answer.'

'Thank you,' said Robobum.

The bum-fighters watched the Great White Bum walk towards the canyon and stand with his back turned to them.

'Well?' said Ned. 'What do you think?'

'I say we play for time,' said Zack. 'The longer we can stall and keep the Great White Bum here, the more likely it is that the arseteroid will hit before he can begin the evacuation.'

'Good plan,' said Ned. 'What do you think, Eleanor?'

'I've got a better idea,' she replied quietly. 'We've got the Great White Bum in front of us. On the edge of a canyon. Unsuspecting and completely helpless. I say we fire Robobum's nuclear wart-head and blast him right over the edge. By the time the Great White Bum realises what's happened he will be splattered all over the rocks at the bottom and he will never trouble us – or the univarse – ever again.'

Ned nodded. 'That sounds like a good plan, too.'

'I don't think so,' said the Mutant Spew Lord.

'Nobody asked you,' said Eleanor.

'Eleanor, I understand your attitude,' said the Mutant Spew Lord. 'But as I sacrificed my life for you – and the cause – I think I have the right to at least be heard.'

'He does have a point,' said Zack.

Eleanor glared at Zack. Then she glared at the Mutant Spew Lord. 'Whatever,' she shrugged.

'Thank you,' said the Mutant Spew Lord, the fingers on his remaining arm trembling slightly. 'I merely wanted to make the point that violence has never worked against the Great White Bum. We all know he is a freak. He's survived a bumcano blast and an interplanetary head-on collision. I tell you, the Great White Bum is indestructible and if you think that a mere fall into a canyon will finish him off, you could be throwing away the best chance we've ever had of ridding the univarse of this menace once and for all.'

'Which is?' said Eleanor.

'Play for time, as Zack suggests,' said the Mutant Spew Lord. 'But don't stay here. Go back with him to the Crack of Doom and make sure he is directly underneath the arseteroid when it hits. Use the nuclear wart-head to immobilise him, by all means, but don't rely on it to destroy him. Let the arseteroid take care of him. This is an arseteroid – you will remember – that is responsible for one of the greatest mass extinctions of all time. If that doesn't finish him off then nothing will. But at least we will have given it our best possible shot. Anything less would be doing a disservice to what is – whether you like to admit it or not – a very worthy adversary.'

Eleanor shook her head. 'There's nothing *worthy* about the Great White Bum,' she said. 'I don't care how indestructible he is or if he does give legless bumantula abdomens to his girlfriends. There's not a single redeeming bone in his horrible detestable flabby cheeks.'

'Bums don't have *any* bones,' said Zack's bum.

'Shut up!' said Eleanor. 'I'm *still* not speaking to you.'

'I think the Mutant Spew Lord has a good point, though,' said Zack. 'Remember how our attempt to destroy the newborn Great White Bum backfired?'

'*Your* attempt,' she said. 'A Great White Bum in the hand is worth millions of Great White Bums at the Crack of Doom. I say we nuclear wart-head him into oblivion right now. While we still can.'

'They are all good plans,' said Ned. 'But much as it pains me to say it, I agree with the Mutant Spew Lord. It's the only absolutely guaranteed way we have of destroying the Great White Bum – not just for now, but for all time.'

'I agree,' said Zack.

'Me too,' said Zack's bum.

'Looks like I'm outvoted,' said Eleanor. 'I just hope you all know what you're doing.'

CHAPTER 58

KISS

The Great White Bum turned and walked back towards Robobum. 'So, my dear, what is your decision?' he said. 'Will you be my bride?'

'What should I tell him?' said Robobum, internally.

'Accept,' said Eleanor, 'but insist on a wedding *before* you leave.'

'Good thinking, Eleanor!' said Ned.

'I accept your offer of marriage,' said Robobum. 'But my honour requires that we marry before we depart for our new kingdom.'

'But,' said the Great White Bum, 'a Great White Bum as beautiful – and rare – as you should have a ceremony fit for a Queen. I suggest we get married in the new world when there will be more time to have the sort of wedding you deserve. A beautiful wedding gown made out of the softest, whitest toilet tissue in the world, a giant fluffy pink toilet-seat cover for your throne, and a bouquet made out of human heads . . .'

'No,' said Robobum. 'I may be a little old-fashioned, but as a single female it wouldn't be right for me to travel with you. If we can't be married first then I must refuse.'

At this the Great White Bum visibly softened.

'But of course,' he said. 'If that is your wish then that is how it shall be. I have spent a lifetime searching for you – I'm not going to let a small detail like this come between us.'

As the Great White Bum spoke he was leaning in closer and closer to Robobum.

'He'll squash the bumantula if he's not careful,' said Ned.

'Is he about to do what I think he's about to do?' said Eleanor.

'What?' said Zack's bum.

'He's going to kiss us!' said Eleanor, her eyes wide.

'Gross!' said Zack's bum, covering its eye with both hands.

But the Great White Bum's cheeks had barely touched Robobum's cheeks when the ground began to shake with a series of violent tremors.

'What's that?' said Zack.

An ear-splitting bellow followed by a series of loud pounding noises disturbed the romantic atmosphere.

'Uh-oh,' said Ned. 'Looks like Romeo's got some competition.'

Zack stared at the awesome creature stamping heavily along the canyon edge towards them.

It was the biggest, chunkiest, most muscle-bound

bum Zack had ever seen. And definitely the ugliest. It was covered in thick black bristly hair, except for a bare leathery patch of skin on each cheek. The hairy beast was beating on these patches with its huge fists and bellowing ferociously.

'Oh no,' said the Great White Bum, pulling away from Robobum. 'Not this *goon*. Not *now*!'

CHAPTER 59

STINK KONG

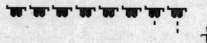

'Who is it?' said Robobum, who had no match-
ing files to help her recognize this terrifying
bumosaur.

'Stink Kong!' said the Great White Bum. 'My old
enemy. Look how the bumnut trees wither and die as
he approaches. He should be ashamed of himself!
What a disgusting pig!'

'That's rich, coming from him,' whispered
Eleanor. 'But then I guess it takes one to know one.'

'I'm sorry, my love,' said the Great White Bum
apologetically to Robobum. 'I'm going to have to
take care of this ugly ape once and for all. Things
could get a little rough. You might like to stand aside
and cover your eye.'

'Whatever you say,' said Robobum. 'Good luck!'

Robobum reversed as far as she could and drew
her hand up across the bumcam concealed on her
roof.

'No!' said Ned. 'Don't do that! We want to watch!'

Robobum obediently parted her fingers.

The fight was already in full swing.

Stink Kong was pounding the Great White Bum like a punchbag. The Great White Bum grabbed Stink Kong in a death-hug and threw him down.

Zack could feel the ground shake, even through Robobum. 'Why doesn't he just gas Stink Kong and get it over with?' said Zack.

'That only works on animals and humans,' said Zack's bum. 'We don't have noses, remember?'

'But what about Stenchgantor?' said Zack. 'It had a nose. I defeated it with a pair of dirty socks!'

'All right, all right, enough already about how you defeated Stenchgantor with your dirty socks,' said Eleanor. 'It was a great achievement, but do you have to go on about it?'

'You're just jealous,' said Zack.

'Yeah, right,' said Eleanor. 'Jealous of your total lack of personal hygiene. I suppose I can only dream of having feet – or a bum – as smelly as yours.'

'Hey!' said Zack's bum. 'That's out of line.'

'So?' said Eleanor. 'What are you going to do about it?'

Zack's bum bent over and was about to zap Eleanor when there was a huge earth-shattering crash.

Zack looked up to see the Great White Bum lying on his back and Stink Kong jumping up and down on him as if he were on a trampoline.

'That Stink Kong is certainly tough,' said Ned. 'But I don't think that using the Great White Bum as a trampoline is such a good idea.'

Suddenly Stink Kong was blown high into the air by a giant brown geyser emitted from the centre of the Great White Bum.

'That's why I didn't think it was a good idea,' said Ned.

Zack heard a hissing sound behind him.

He turned and saw the Mutant Spew Lord totally engrossed in the fight, punching the air with his remaining arm and hissing, 'Yesss!'

Then, without warning, Robobum began to rise into the air.

'Robobum?' said Ned. 'What are you doing? I didn't tell you to lift off!'

'Negative,' said Robobum. 'Robobum is not lifting off. Robobum is being carried away by a large bumodactyl.'

'Oh, great!' said Ned. '*Bumodactyls*. That's all we need!'

CHAPTER 60

BUMODACTYL

Within moments Stink Kong and the Great White Bum were just tiny figures sparring on the far side of the canyon, a long, long way beneath them.

'Activate thrusters, Robobum!' said Ned.

'Negative,' said Robobum. 'Thrusters are not responding.'

'Turbo-assisted jet-repulsion unit!' yelled Ned.

'Negative,' said Robobum. 'Turbo-assisted jet-repulsion unit damaged by the bumantula.'

'Have you got anything?' said Ned through gritted teeth. 'Anything at all?'

'Of course,' said Robobum. 'I have onboard tea-and coffee-making facilities. Would you like milk with that, madam? Sugar? One lump or two thousand? Yes, it is a very nice day. I am Robobum. Ro-bo-bum. RO. BO. BUM. WITH. MILK.'

'What's going on, Ned?' said Zack. 'What's wrong with Robobum?'

'Poor old girl, she's been knocked around a bit too much,' said Ned. 'Sounds like her higher speech and thinking functions have been scrambled, and her thrusters and turbo are out of action.'

'Is there anything we can do?' said Eleanor, staring at the bumcam image of the bumodactyl's leathery cheek-wings as they pushed down on either side of the screen.

'I don't think so,' said Ned, studying his *What Bumosaur is That?* book. 'Bumodactyls are powerful. Says here an adult bumodactyl can have a wingspan of up to fifty metres. Its wings are made of a membrane that stretches from its finger to its back legs. And they're methane assisted!'

'A brilliant design!' hissed the Mutant Spew Lord.

'When we want the opinion of a mutant we'll ask for it,' said Eleanor coldly.

'Some of them are toothless,' said Ned, still reading from his book, 'while others have hundreds of bristle-like teeth lining their long, razor-sharp beaks . . .'

'Ned,' said Eleanor. 'Thanks for the lecture. It's truly fascinating. But what I want to know is, can we fire something at it?'

'I'm afraid not,' said Ned. 'The bumodactyl is directly above us. There is no artillery in the roof.'

'It doesn't matter,' said the Mutant Spew Lord. 'I wouldn't give up on the Great White Bum yet. He won't abandon Robobum that easily. He'll save us.'

'You sound like you're on his side,' said Eleanor suspiciously.

The Mutant Spew Lord laughed. 'Once upon a

time,' he said. 'But no more. Anybody can make a mistake.'

Eleanor stared at the sad heap of flesh and sticks and leaves in front of her.

'Body?' she said. 'You call that a *body*?'

Zack groaned. 'Uh-oh,' he said. 'That doesn't look good.'

'You're telling me,' said Eleanor.

'No,' said Zack. 'Look at the screen.'

Eleanor looked at the screen. They were flying towards an enormous bumcano. The bumcano was ringed by an impressive collar of sheer black stone rising many thousands of metres straight up. It made the Great White Bum's bumcano look like an anthill.

As they drew closer, the bum-fighters could see bumodactyl nests wedged in among the ledges of the rock-face.

And, even more worryingly, they could see the heads of hungry bumodactyl chicks eagerly poking out of the nests, opening and closing their razor-edged cheeks.

'I never thought I'd hear myself saying this,' said Zack, 'but I hope the Great White Bum gets here soon.'

CHAPTER 61

NEST

The bumodactyl flew up the face of the bumcano. It flew until it had reached almost the highest point, where the rock met the smoking mouth of the vent. There, in a nest so large that it looked as if it was constructed out of tree trunks, were more bumodactyl chicks.

Three of them – each a rusty red colour. And each with a razor-sharp beak.

They were so excited by the arrival of their meal that they were practically leaping out of the nest.

'So, what's our plan?' said Zack.

Ned laughed without humour. 'Plan? That assumes that we knew this was going to happen. I'm not too worried about the chicks. I doubt they'll be able to do much damage to Robobum's exterior . . .'

'Famous last words,' said Eleanor. 'That's what you said about the bumantula, and look what happened.'

'Fair go, Eleanor,' said Ned. 'I'm doing my best.

This isn't easy for anybody, you know. We're all in uncharted territory here.'

'I'm sorry,' said Eleanor, biting her fingernail. 'I guess the thought of becoming a bumodactyl snack has got me a little tense.'

'I don't think you're going to have to worry about that,' said Zack's bum as the bumodactyl placed Robobum down on a ledge, a short distance above the nest. 'At least not for a little while.'

'So, we're not going to be eaten?' said Zack.

'Not yet,' said Zack's bum. 'Looks like they're starting with an entrée.'

Eleanor peered at the image of the nest on bum-cam . . . and screamed. The bumodactyl that had brought them there was dangling a small pink bum above her babies' beaks.

'Aaaggghh!' screamed the helpless bum.

'That's my bum!' yelled Eleanor, leaping to her feet. 'I've got to save it!'

'Don't be a fool!' said Zack.

'Look who's talking,' said Eleanor. 'You'd save your bum if it was down there, wouldn't you?'

Zack looked at the wildly snapping beaks of the bumodactyls and hesitated.

'Well?' said his bum. 'Wouldn't you?'

Zack looked at his bum. And then back at the bumodactyls. And then back at his bum. 'I suppose so,' said Zack, uncertainly. 'But those things will eat you alive!'

'Better that than knowing I didn't try to save my bum when I had the chance,' said Eleanor, already standing in the teleport beam.

Zack sighed. 'Hang on,' he said. 'I'll come with you.'

'Be careful, Zack,' said his bum.

'Of course,' said Zack. '"Careful" is my middle name.'

'No, it's not,' said his bum. 'It's Henry.'

'Shush,' said Zack. 'I thought I told you never to say that ever again.'

'Sorry, Zack,' said his bum. 'Your secret's safe with me.'

'And me,' said Eleanor.

'And me,' smirked Ned.

'And me,' said the Mutant Spew Lord, making a sound somewhere between laughter and throwing up. But whatever sound it was, Zack Henry Freeman didn't like it.

CHAPTER 62

SNATCH!

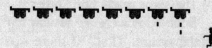

Zack and Eleanor teleported on to the ledge of the bumcano.

The bumodactyl nest was about 10 metres below them.

Eleanor pulled a roll of triple-strength toilet paper from her bum-fighter utility belt.

She wrapped a length around her waist and knotted it tightly. She then handed the roll to Zack. 'Let it out slowly,' she yelled against the roar of the wind, 'and get a good grip on the rock-face. You may have to take my whole weight.'

'OK!' yelled Zack. 'Be careful.'

'No time for that,' called Eleanor as she launched herself backwards over the ledge and abseiled down a narrow crevice. The bumodactyl was perched on the edge of the nest with its back to her. It had Eleanor's bum in its beak, but seemed unable to decide which of the screaming chicks to give the prize to.

Zack bit his lip.

It was scary up on the ledge.

In the sky above him he could see the menacing glow of the approaching arseteroid. It was noticeably bigger now and getting larger by the second.

And down below – way down below – he could see a prehistoric stink bog.

The sight made him shiver.

Stink bogs were a one-way trip to fossil museums of the future. That's if there *was* a future for fossil museums to exist in, thought Zack grimly.

Once a bumosaur – or a person for that matter – got stuck in a stink bog, that was it. The rotting matter was so thick and sticky that nothing could escape it. With great difficulty, Zack tore his gaze – and his thoughts – away from the stink bog and looked down to check on Eleanor's progress.

She was almost three-quarters of the way down the crevice to the nest. But then the bumodactyl looked back and noticed her.

Out of sheer surprise it opened its beak and dropped Eleanor's bum, which fell into the beak of the closest chick. The mother squawked a loud warning rasp at Eleanor.

'That's exactly how I feel about you, too,' said Eleanor as she leaped from the wall and swung – Tarzan style – over the top of the nest. Reaching down as she swept past, she plucked her bum out of the bumodactyl chick's beak. Then she swung upward into the sky.

'Eleanor?' said her bum, who was dazed and almost blue from the cold.

'Don't worry,' said Eleanor, hugging her bum to her chest. 'I've got you. And I'm not letting go . . . whether you like it or not!'

'I like it . . .' said her bum, as Eleanor reached the furthermost point of her swing.

But their ordeal was not over yet.

They now had to swing back through a gauntlet of enraged bumodactyl chicks and their super-enraged bumodactyl mother.

Eleanor took a deep breath, gripped the toilet paper extra hard and let out a banshee scream that her father had taught her.

The bumodactyls were too stunned to snap at her as she swooped past.

'Great going, Eleanor,' said her bum.

'Thanks,' said Eleanor as she gripped the rock-face and, helped by her bum, began climbing back up to the ledge.

CHAPTER 63

PANIC

Zack hauled in the toilet paper as fast as he could. He was looking out straight ahead of him — trying not to look down — when he saw a familiar shape flying through the air towards them.

The Great White Bum!

'Hurry, Eleanor!' yelled Zack.

'What do you think I'm doing?' she said. 'I'm going as fast as I can.'

'Look behind you,' said Zack.

Eleanor glanced over her shoulder. She knew as well as Zack that it would be disastrous for the Great White Bum to catch them out here. If he realised that Robobum was a machine, their whole plan would come unravelled in an instant.

Zack was really sweating now.

The Great White Bum was getting closer.

And to make things worse, the mother bumodactyl was heading their way to retrieve the bum that had been stolen from her.

The fossil museum of the future was looking more and more like a real possibility with every passing second.

Zack imagined his bones being excavated from the stink bog.

The bones would be labelled and put into a glass case.

Maybe they'd even be assembled and motorised and hooked up to a button on the outside of the case for snotty schoolkids to push and laugh at as his bones jiggled around.

The bumodactyl was swooping and snapping at the toilet paper. One of the perforations began to tear apart.

'Faster!' yelled Zack, grimacing as he strained to pull Eleanor up the mountain. 'The Great White Bum is almost here!'

Suddenly Eleanor's bum appeared . . . and then Eleanor's head.

She reached up and Zack pulled them both on to the ledge beside him, almost crying with relief.

'Come on,' he said, 'let's get back into Robobum while we still have time.'

They clambered up and into Robobum's teleportation beam.

The bumodactyl swooped in for a final desperate attempt to retrieve Eleanor's bum. This time Eleanor's bum joined Eleanor in a banshee scream that scared the bumodactyl rigid and sent the unfortunate creature plummeting over the ledge and down towards the stink bog below.

But despite whatever humiliating fate was in store for it in the future, it received no sympathy from the bum-fighters, who were already teleporting back to the relative safety of Robobum.

Or so they thought.

CHAPTER 64
SKULLDUGGERY

As Zack rematerialised inside Robobum, he could
tell something was wrong. Exactly what, however-
er, he couldn't quite put his finger on.

Was it the fact that Ned was lying, face down, in a
pool of blood?

Or was it the fact that the Mutant Spew Lord
was sitting in a chair with a bum-gun pointed at
them?

Zack thought quickly – well, as quickly as you can
in the middle of a state of total confusion – and came
to the conclusion that it was both of these things put
together.

Something was most definitely – and most horribly
– wrong. As wrong as something most definitely and
most horribly wrong could possibly be.

'Welcome back,' said the Mutant Spew Lord. 'But
I'm afraid there's been a little accident.'

'What have you done, you putrid piece of slime?'
said Eleanor, staring in shock at Ned's body.

'Well,' said the Mutant Spew Lord, 'there was a slight difference of opinion between myself and Ned while you were out and . . .'

'You *shot* Ned!' said Eleanor.

' "Shot" is a very strong word,' said the Mutant Spew Lord.

'But it's the *right* word,' said Eleanor.

'I had no choice,' said the Mutant Spew Lord. 'He was threatening the success of the mission!'

'Ned *was* the mission!' yelled Zack, blinking back tears. 'He *built* Robobum. He rescued us. If it wasn't for him, none of us would even be here!'

'No,' said the Mutant Spew Lord. 'And if he'd had his way, none of you would be here now. He wanted to just fly away and leave you.'

'Ned would never do a thing like that,' said Eleanor. 'You haven't changed at all. You're still a liar. And a lousy one. And besides, if you're so interested in our welfare, why are you pointing a gun at us?'

The Mutant Spew Lord shifted uncomfortably. 'Because I rather suspected that you wouldn't believe my side of the story and that you might try to do something silly.'

'Why don't we ask Robobum?' said Eleanor.

'I'm afraid that won't be possible,' said the Mutant Spew Lord. 'She is having a little sleep.'

'We're under manual control?' said Zack.

'No, you fool,' said the Mutant Spew Lord coldly. 'You're under *my* control.'

Zack looked into the Mutant Spew Lord's eyes. As the Kisser, the Mutant Spew Lord had switched allegiance from the bum-fighters to the bums. As the Mutant Zombie Maggot Lord he'd switched allegiance from the bums to his beloved maggots and then finally back to the bum-fighters. Now it seemed he had switched allegiance once again.

Slowly, as Zack stared into the depths of the Mutant Spew Lord's vacant eyes, he realised the truth. The Mutant Spew Lord's true allegiance was to nobody but himself. He was interested only in power. *Absolute power*. And if that came at the cost of the survival of the human race, then that was a price the Mutant Spew Lord was willing to pay. Even his apparent selflessness in sacrificing himself to the mutant maggots was probably a purely selfish act: part of a desperate – but calculated – strategy to transform himself yet again in his endless, insatiable quest for power. Nothing – and nobody – else mattered. Not Ned, not Eleanor, not Zack and not . . .

'Oh no!' said Zack. 'Where's my bum? What have you done with my bum? I swear, if you've hurt it—'

Suddenly there was an almighty jolt as Robobum rose into the air again.

But not under her own power.

She was now being rocked none too gently in the Great White Bum's arms.

'Sorry about that, my love,' said the Great White Bum in a soothing voice as they took off. 'But don't worry. Neither Stink Kong nor the bumodactyl will

CHAPTER 65

DESTINY?

Meanwhile, on board Robobum, all hell had broken loose. The sudden movement had caused the bum-fighters to lose their footing and fall to the ground in a sprawling heap. Eleanor landed first. Her bum fell on top of her. Zack landed on top of her and then his bum fell on top of them all.

'Where did you come from?' said Zack, overjoyed to see his bum again.

'I was hiding in the roof,' said his bum. 'Hiding from *him*!' Zack's bum pointed at the Mutant Spew Lord, who, being more liquid than solid, hadn't been affected by the upheaval. 'He went crazy! He killed Ned!'

'We know,' said Zack, patting his bum.

'Ned was getting ready to fire Robobum's nuclear wart-head at the Great White Bum,' said Zack's bum.

'Why?' said Eleanor.

'To protect you and Zack,' said Zack's bum. 'He

was worried that the Great White Bum was going to see you. And then the Mutant Spew Lord went crazy. He grabbed a bum-gun and shot Ned in the back. Then he tried to kill me, but I ran away and hid.'

'That sounds more like the Kisser that I've come to know and despise,' said Eleanor grimly. 'Just you wait. By the time I get through with you, you're going to wish you'd never reconstituted yourself. You're going to wish you'd never crawled out of the brown lake alive. In fact, you're going to wish that you'd never been born.'

'I'm not sure that hurting me is such a good idea,' said the Mutant Spew Lord. 'Stop and *think* about it. You're a smart girl, Eleanor. Headstrong, but smart. No matter what you do to me – or *think* you want to do to me – the Great White Bum's rise is inevitable and we have the perfect opportunity to take advantage of it.'

'There's nothing "inevitable" about the Great White Bum's rise,' said Eleanor. 'We can still stop him!'

'But why would you *want* to stop him?' said the Mutant Spew Lord. 'Don't you see? This is what was prophesied in *The Book of Bumageddon*! I am doing nothing more than helping destiny to fulfil itself.'

Eleanor spat. 'There's no such thing as *destiny*,' she said. 'It's not a place or a foregone conclusion. We're making it up as we go along, and we can work towards a better world or a world of Bumageddon – it's our choice – *your* choice – *right now*!'

'But that's my point exactly,' said the Mutant Spew Lord. 'With the aid of Robobum we can rule the world alongside the Great White Bum! That opportunity doesn't come along every day, you know. By defeating the Great White Bum now, we ultimately lose – we become nobodies with no power – but if we help the Great White Bum, we win – *we win the world.*'

'You mutated piece of mutant zombie blowfly spew,' said Eleanor, walking towards the Mutant Spew Lord with her hands outstretched. 'Give me the gun. Your dirty double-crossing treachery ends here.'

'You want to talk about dirty double-crossing treachery?' said the Mutant Spew Lord. 'Let's start with you riding around in a robotic bum making promises of marriage that you have no intention of keeping! I would have thought that qualified as dirty double-crossing treachery on at least two counts: pretending to be what you are not and intended breach of promise.'

Eleanor stared at the Mutant Spew Lord, her eyes cold. 'I never said I was perfect.'

'Neither did I,' said the Mutant Spew Lord, raising the bum-gun.

'No, Eleanor!' said Zack. 'Stop! He's deranged. He'll do it!'

'Zack's right,' said the Mutant Spew Lord. 'I will.'

But Eleanor didn't say a word. She just continued walking towards him.

Zack saw the Mutant Spew Lord's finger twitch on the trigger.

There was a blast of light and an incredible noise as three rounds of atomic bum-blasting bullets leaped from the mouth of the gun.

CHAPTER 66

PRAYERS

'Eeergggh!' said a voice.

But it wasn't Eleanor.

It was her bum.

At the crucial moment it had leaped in front of the Mutant Spew Lord's bum-gun and was now rolling around on the ground clutching its cheeks.

Eleanor fixed the surprised Mutant Spew Lord with a look of deadly intent and tore the gun from his hand, raised it to her shoulder and pointed it at his head. Or, at least, what passed for his head.

He shielded himself weakly with his remaining arm, or, at least, what passed for his remaining arm.

'You can mess with me all you like,' said Eleanor, 'but nobody messes with my bum! Say your prayers, mutant – if there's a god mutated enough to hear them . . .'

'Negative,' said Robobum, crackling back to life. 'I have checked my data banks. There is no god *that* mutated.'

'Thanks, Robobum,' said Zack, who had taken advantage of the commotion to reactivate Robobum.

'Guess it's just not your lucky day,' said Eleanor to the Mutant Spew Lord as she squeezed the trigger.

Zack closed his eyes.

CHAPTER 67

HOUSEKEEPING

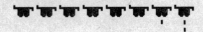

When Zack opened his eyes, he was amazed to see that nothing had changed.

The Mutant Spew Lord was still sitting in his chair.

Eleanor was still standing in front of him with the gun.

And a glance out of the window indicated that they were still speeding towards the Crack of Doom.

'The Mutant Spew Lord is still alive,' said Robobum. 'Status report indicates the Mutant Spew Lord's body density is a mere one per cent – in other words, he is ninety-nine per cent flesh-free. The bullets have passed through him with little impact.'

'Wish you'd told me that before,' said Eleanor.

'You didn't ask,' said Robobum.

'OK,' said Eleanor. 'I'm asking now. How do we get rid of this piece of bullet-proof slime?'

'Removal of onboard slime best achieved by activation of wet and dry suction unit located in hall cupboard,' said Robobum.

The Mutant Spew Lord looked horrified.

'No,' he said. 'You wouldn't . . . not the vacuum cleaner!'

'I'm afraid so,' said Zack, retrieving the unit from the cupboard. 'You leave us no choice.'

Zack switched it on.

The high-pitched suction unit roared into life.

The Mutant Spew Lord cowered in terror and started to slide across the floor and into a crevice.

'Quick, Zack!' yelled Eleanor. 'He's getting away!'

Zack just smiled and fixed a crevice attachment to the end of the hose.

The Mutant Spew Lord screamed. Or, at least, made a noise that might have passed for a scream if anyone had been able to hear it above the vacuum cleaner's roar.

Schluuurrrrpp!

Within a moment the Mutant Spew Lord had disappeared up the deadly nozzle – his watery flesh no match for the awesome power of the heavy-duty bum-fighting vacuum cleaner.

Eleanor looked at the ex-Mutant Spew Lord, now just a thin watery puddle of blood and rotting flesh in the bottom of the transparent hard plastic vacuum-cleaner body.

'Good work, Zack,' said Eleanor.

Zack, who was staring at the brown mush, hoped she was right.

He could see one of the Mutant Spew Lord's eyeballs floating in the middle of the liquefied remains – and worse still, it was staring back at him.

Zack shivered and turned away.

He looked across to where Eleanor's bum lay and saw his bum jumping up and down on top of it.

'What do you think you're doing?' said Zack.

'Bum-to-bum resuscitation,' said Zack's bum.

'No!' said Eleanor, rushing across the room. 'You'll kill her!'

'She was *already* dead,' said Zack's bum. 'It's worth a try!'

Suddenly Eleanor's bum groaned.

Eleanor knelt down beside the two bums. 'She's alive?' she said to Zack's bum.

'Yes,' said Zack's bum, hopping off.

'Thank you,' said Eleanor. 'I'll take over now.'

Zack's bum nodded gravely and stepped back.

Eleanor picked up her wounded bum and cradled it gently in her arms. 'How are you feeling?' she said.

'Just a flesh wound,' said her bum. 'I developed a pretty thick hide out there in the jungle. I had to. I've suffered worse.'

'You saved my life,' said Eleanor.

'You saved mine,' said Eleanor's bum. 'It was the least I could do.'

Eleanor bit her lip. 'I'm really sorry,' she said. 'The last few years must have been very hard for you. I don't know how I'll ever make it up to you.'

'It's OK,' said her bum. 'You just did.'

CHAPTER 68
FAREWELL

The mood inside Robobum was sombre as Zack and his bum dragged Ned Smelly's body to the area underneath the teleportation beam. Zack folded Ned's arms across his chest and placed his home-made metal helmet on his head.

'Ned was one of the best,' said Zack. 'Without him none of this would have been possible.'

Tears came to Zack's eyes as he thought about how much they owed Ned. It was Ned who had rescued them from certain death after their crash-landing in the Great Windy Desert many adventures ago. And it was Ned who had rescued them from the Kisser's treachery on the bumcano. And, of course, more recently, it was Ned who had rescued them from Bumageddon.

'He was a good man,' said Eleanor, looking up from her bum. 'I never heard him say a bad thing about anybody.'

'Or any *bum*,' said Zack's bum. 'He was always

kind to me. Even though he was a bum-fighter he was always kind.'

'He was the best inventor a robotic bum could have wanted,' said Robobum quietly.

Zack stepped back with his head bowed. 'May your bum be with you,' he said solemnly. 'OK, Robobum . . . take him up.'

Robobum's teleportation beam glowed and Ned's body began to grow faint.

Suddenly Zack ran to the other side of the room. 'Hang on, Robobum!'

Zack returned with Ned's *What Bumosaur is That?* and placed it on top of his almost transparent body. 'I think he'd appreciate that,' said Zack.

'So do I,' said Robobum.

CHAPTER 69

CRACK

Nobody spoke much as the Great White Bum carried them towards the Crack of Doom. The only sounds were the small whimpers of pain from Eleanor's bum as Eleanor dabbed at her wounds with cotton wool soaked in antiseptic.

'I'm sorry,' said Eleanor, after each dab. 'I'm sorry.'

'It's all right,' said Eleanor's bum. 'I know you don't mean to hurt me.'

Zack's bum wiped a tear from its eye and joined Zack, who was gazing at the bumcam screen.

Together they watched as the Great White Bum descended towards an enormous jagged smoking gash in the ground. They felt as if they were looking directly down into the very bowels of the earth.

It was not a pretty sight.

Suddenly Zack's thoughts flashed back to his traumatic experiences inside the bumcano.

The brown lake.

The maggots.

The Great White Bum.

The match.

The gas.

The death stink.

The explosion.

But this was worse.

The sheer enormity of the Crack of Doom made the brown lake look like a harmless puddle.

The Great White Bum set Robobum down gently.

'Destination reached,' said Robobum. 'Prepare for wedding ceremony.'

Zack and Eleanor looked across the room at each other. In a desperate mission already packed with danger, they both knew that this was the most dangerous part of all.

They looked at the screen.

And gasped.

Giant brown blobs were flying in all directions.

They were surrounded by thousands of Great White Bums.

Hundreds of thousands of Great White Bums.

Hundreds of thousands of Great White Bums involved in a free-for-all riot.

Somehow Robobum – no matter how technologically advanced – didn't seem like much protection against an entire colony of Great White Bums.

CHAPTER 70

TEARS

'Here we are,' said the Great White Bum. 'The Crack of Doom. My home. My subjects. Your subjects-to-be.'

As the Great White Bum said this, all the Great White Bums immediately stopped their fighting and turned to their master. A ripple of excitement ran through the crowd.

'As you already know, our departure time is soon – very soon – but first I have an announcement,' said the Great White Bum. 'After a lifetime of searching for a bum as great and as white as myself I have finally found her. She is to be my wife and your Queen. A fitting way to start our new world order!'

There was a roar of approval from the bums.

'Come, my bride,' said the Great White Bum. 'Give me your hand. It is time for us to be married.'

Robobum obediently extended her hand.

'What do you think we should do?' said Eleanor. 'Should we detonate the nuclear wart-head?'

'No,' said Zack. 'It's still too early. We have to slow things down. If the marriage happens too quickly they'll leave before the arseteroid hits. We have to stall for as long as possible until it's too late for the bums to evacuate. We need to make sure the Great White Bum is underneath that arseteroid. Then we can time travel back to safety at the absolute last second.'

'How do I do this?' said Robobum, using her inside voice.

'Tell him you can't get married without a dress,' said Eleanor's bum.

'Great idea,' said Eleanor. 'And flowers!'

'And music!' said Zack's bum.

Robobum turned to the Great White Bum. 'I'm really very excited about getting married,' she said, sweetly. 'But I need a dress. And flowers. And music.'

'But, my dear,' said the Great White Bum, flushing crimson with impatience. 'We must get married now. Dresses and flowers and music . . . these things take time to prepare. Time that we can barely afford, my darling. We must be off the planet before the arseteroid strikes. There is less time than you think.'

Suddenly the bum-fighters were thrown to the ground as huge tremors shook Robobum.

'What's happening?' said Zack, desperately trying to find something to grab on to.

'I don't know,' said Eleanor. 'If I didn't know that Robobum was just a machine I'd say she was . . . she was *crying*.'

'Crying?' said Zack. 'But that's impossible. She can't . . . unless . . . hang on . . . that's brilliant!'

'What?' said Eleanor. 'What's brilliant?'

'Listen!' said Zack. 'She's *pretending*.'

'Don't cry, my sweet,' said the Great White Bum, patting Robobum gently. 'Please don't cry. Of course you shall have these things. Anything you desire will be yours. A beautiful dress. The best flowers that have evolved so far, and music so sweet you'll think it was blown from the cheeks of the bum-angels themselves.'

The Great White Bums stood motionless, staring at the sight of their Queen-to-be sobbing.

'Well?' said the Great White Bum to his subjects. 'What are you oafs waiting for?' He pointed at three bums. 'You, you and you! Get my Queen a dress, flowers and music. Hop to it!'

'Great!' said Zack, excited at the success of their plan. 'That should keep them busy for ages. It should be near impossible to find those things in this world.'

'Yes, good work, Robobum,' said Eleanor. 'You're a smooth operator.'

'Smooth operator?' said Robobum. 'What is "smooth operator"?'

'Using tears to get the Great White Bum to do what you want!' said Eleanor.

'Using tears?' said Robobum. 'I wasn't "using" them . . . I was really upset. I want my wedding to be special.'

'Of course,' said Zack, shooting a look of concern at Eleanor. 'Of course! What bum wouldn't?'

'Thank you, Zack,' said Robobum. 'I only wish my

creator, Ned Smelly, was alive to give me away. He was like a father to me.' Robobum started to cry again.

'Yes,' said Zack, worried at how seriously Robobum seemed to be taking the wedding. 'I'm sure Ned would have liked that.'

CHAPTER 71

WRONG!

Z ack looked into the sky.
    The arseteroid was close now.

Very close.

He clenched his fists.

The future of the world depended on the next two hours.

This was it.

This was what all the bum-kicking, bum-smacking, bum-pinching, bum-forking, bum-flicking and bum-fighting – real and simulated – had been leading up to.

The final pongflict.

It had been a long and smelly road.

Across the Great Windy Desert. Through the Brown Forest. Over the Sea of Bums. Into the heart of a bumcano. Caught in a simulated crapalanche. Trapped inside an underground maggotorium. Sucked into a brown hole. Lost on Uranus. Buried under a giant brown blob.

But the long and smelly road was almost at an end.

Zack sucked in a deep breath as he summoned up the courage, the energy and the resolve for the battle that would determine the very course of bumolution.

Despite the Blind Bum-feeler's predictions that Zack would be the saviour of free men everywhere, Zack had seen and experienced too much to think that success was guaranteed. The Great White Bum was a powerful foe. And most of the cards were stacked in the Great White Bum's favour.

Zack was certain, however, that Robobum's wedding demands would prove impossible to fulfil, thus buying them the time they needed to launch the nuclear wart-head, immobilise the Great White Bum and ensure that the giant arseteroid would put an end to both him and his deranged dream of world domination.

This was, after all, a world in which wedding dresses hadn't yet been invented. A world in which flowers were a relatively new – and therefore scarce – bumolutionary product.

And, surely, the chance that 'sweet' music could exist in such a world was remote.

But Zack was wrong.

Wrong on all three counts.

CHAPTER 72

AWOL

Within an hour the three Great White Bums returned bearing their precious gifts.

The first bum to approach the Great White Bum bowed and scraped the ground.

'I bring a most beautiful dress for your bride,' it said as it knelt and held out the white paper-thin bark of a primitive bum-tree.

Robobum gasped with pleasure at the sight of it. 'It's beautiful,' she said, wrapping it around herself like a sarong.

She turned slowly from side to side. 'Does my bum – I mean – do *I* look too big in this?' she said to the Great White Bum.

'No. It's perfect,' said the Great White Bum. 'You look even more beautiful than before.'

'You're sure I don't look fat?' said Robobum. 'I wish I had time to lose just a few kilos.'

'Robobum seems to be really getting into this "wedding" thing,' said Eleanor quietly to Zack.

'I'm hoping it's just an act,' said Zack.

'Me too,' said Eleanor, biting her lip.

'It *is* a beautiful dress,' said Eleanor's bum.

The second Great White Bum stepped forward with a very impressive bouquet of ferns and grasses that, while not technically flowers, were still very pretty.

They heard Robobum gasp again, and she brought the plants up to her face as if to smell them.

'Olfactory report indicates molecular breakdown very pleasant . . .' said Robobum.

'What's that, my dear?' said the Great White Bum.

'Robobum!' whispered Zack. 'Stop doing Robospeak!'

'Sorry,' said Robobum. 'It's just that they're *so* beautiful!'

Again Zack and Eleanor traded worried glances. What was happening to Robobum? She was the onboard computer of a bum-fighting machine, programmed for functionality and practicality. She wasn't set up to appreciate beauty or fashion. What would have been the point? But here she was, apparently breathless with excitement about wedding dresses and flowers . . . Zack frowned.

Something wasn't quite right.

But there wasn't time to fix it now.

The third bum stepped up.

'Your Great Whiteness,' it said, 'I present to you the finest wind ensemble in the land. The incomparable, the one and only, Great White Bum Quartet.'

Four Great White Bums stepped forward and

started making the most unpleasant music that Zack had ever heard.

'That is *so* bad,' said Zack.

'Just be grateful that we're in here,' said Eleanor. 'It probably smells even worse than it sounds.'

'I reckon it rocks,' said Zack's bum.

'Yeah,' said Eleanor's bum, who was now recovered enough to sway slowly from side to side and tap its foot. 'It's got a good beat and you can dance to it.'

'It's beautiful,' said Robobum, beginning to cry again.

'So there you have it,' said the Great White Bum. 'A gorgeous dress – a bridal bouquet – and fine music – all you desired – all you deserved and more – now can we get married?'

'No!' said Zack, desperately trying to think of another demand. 'Say no!'

There was a long silence.

'Well?' said the Great White Bum.

'You heard Zack, Robobum,' said Eleanor. 'Tell him no!'

'Oh *yes*,' said Robobum. 'We can get married now. I have everything I need.'

'Oh *no*!' said Zack. 'She ignored our commands!'

'Can we take manual control?' said Eleanor. 'Try the override.'

Zack pushed the button frantically. 'No response,' he said. 'Robobum's gone AWOL!'*

* AWOL: Arse without leave.

CHAPTER 73

WEDDING

Z ack and Eleanor watched helplessly as the Great White Bum led Robobum to stand beside him with her back to the assembled bums.

They watched as two small – and strangely familiar – bums appeared in front of them.

'Isn't that . . .' said Eleanor, trying to remember where she'd seen the bums before. 'Isn't that *the Prince*?'

'And Maurice!' said Zack's bum.

'Who are they?' said Eleanor's bum.

'Good question,' said Zack. 'I'm not sure that they know the answer themselves. One minute they're working for the Great White Bum, next minute they're working against him. Looks like they've gone back to working with him.'

'But why?' said Eleanor.

'Why not?' shrugged Zack. 'Everyone else seems to be.'

'I'm not working for the Great White Bum,' said Zack's bum.

'Me neither,' said Eleanor's bum.

Zack's bum shuffled nervously in her direction. 'Um,' it said, 'I suppose I owe you an apology.'

'It's OK,' said Eleanor's bum. 'You weren't to know.'

'Yes,' said Zack's bum, 'but that doesn't make it—'

'Shush,' said Zack. 'It's starting!'

'Sorry,' said the two bums in unison.

As they watched, the Prince cleared his throat and began to speak. 'We are gathered here today to join these two bums in holy buttrimony.'

'Holy buttrimony,' echoed Maurice. 'Holy, holy buttrimony . . . holy, holy, holy . . .'

'That's enough, Maurice,' said the Prince.

Zack bit his lip.

It was all happening too fast.

'We've got to do something!' said Zack. 'At this rate they'll have married and left for their honeymoon before the arseteroid has even entered the Earth's atmosphere.'

'We've got to launch the nuclear wart-head now,' said Eleanor. 'Hopefully, it will immobilise the Great White Bum and keep him here until the arseteroid hits. We'll do it when they kiss. It's our only chance.'

'You're right,' said Zack. 'I just hope we *can* launch it. Without Robobum's cooperation it may be difficult. And that's assuming it's even functional.'

'I'll get out there and launch the darn thing myself if I have to,' said Eleanor, her eyes burning.

'If there is anybody here who knows why these two bums should not be joined in holy buttrimony,' said the Prince, 'let him speak now or forever hold his peace.'

'Or forever hold his peace,' said Maurice. 'Or forever, and ever and ever . . .'

'Shut up, Maurice!' said the Prince.

'Sorry,' said Maurice.

A hush descended upon the crowd. The Prince waited, but nobody spoke.

'Get on with it,' said the Great White Bum impatiently.

'Yes, Your Whiteness,' said the Prince. 'If there is nobody here who objects, then we may proceed—'

'*I* object!' gurgled a strange and unearthly voice. 'This wedding must not go ahead!'

CHAPTER 74

SPRUNG!

There was a collective intake of breath from the assembled crowd.

Zack and Eleanor both gasped. It was a voice that they knew all too well. It was also a voice that neither of them had expected to hear again. Zack looked over his shoulder at the vacuum cleaner.

It was empty.

All that remained of the Mutant Spew Lord was a glistening trail across the floor which ended at the entrance to the teleportation tube.

'Oh no,' said Zack quietly. 'We're in trouble. BIG trouble. The Mutant Spew Lord must have taken advantage of his liquefied state to escape out of the vacuum cleaner!'

'You're right!' said Eleanor, pointing to the screen. 'Look!'

The wedding crowd was in uproar.

'Who – and what – are you?' thundered the Great White Bum, staring down at the Mutant Spew Lord, who was now little more than a lumpy puddle on the ground in front of him.

'Just a humble servant, Your Whiteness,' said the Mutant Spew Lord puddle. 'One that simply wants – and has always wanted – the best for you.'

'On what grounds, puddle of vomit,' said the Prince, trying to regain control of the proceedings, 'do you object to this wedding taking place?'

'Because,' said the Mutant Spew Lord puddle with a dramatic pause, 'because the bride is not in fact a bum. She is a robot! She is nothing more than a hotted-up bum-mobile!'

There was a collective outpouring of methane from the shocked crowd.

But no bum released more methane than the Great White Bum himself.

'What's the Mutant Spew Lord playing at?' said Eleanor.

'Revenge,' said Zack. 'He must have decided that if he can't have what he wanted, then neither can we.'

The Great White Bum, blanched and shell-shocked, turned to his bride. 'Tell me it's not true!' he begged her. 'Tell me it's not true and I'll have this . . . this . . .'

'Faithful servant,' ventured the Mutant Spew Lord puddle helpfully.

'*Whatever it is*,' continued the Great White Bum, 'scraped up and thrown into the Crack of Doom! Are you really a robot?'

'Tell him it's not true,' Eleanor urged Robobum in the desperate hope that Robobum might have regained control of her higher logic functions. 'Run while you still can!'

'But this is my wedding,' said Robobum in a halting, confused voice.

'It will be your funeral if you don't run while you've still got the chance,' said Eleanor. 'Please!'

The Great White Bum repeated his question. 'Are you really a robot?'

'Affirmative,' said Robobum. 'The puddle of regurgitated zombie blowfly vomit speaks the truth. I am Robobum. Fully riveted reinforced steel cheeks. Turbo-assisted jet-repulsion units. Nuclear warthead equipped. Matter transport assisted entry and exit. Inside and outside voice options. Onboard tea- and coffee-making facilities. And I am self-wiping!'

The Great White Bum let out a bum-wrenching howl of pure pain. 'No!' he cried. 'Tell me it's not true!'

'I cannot deny the truth,' said Robobum. 'But this doesn't have to change anything, does it?'

'Of course it does!' thundered the Great White Bum. 'It changes *everything*. And somebody's going to pay!'

And saying this, the Great White Bum picked Robobum up by the legs, held her upside down and began shaking her violently.

'Uh-oh,' said Zack. 'Hold on, everybody. This could get a little rough.'

But it was too late.

And more than a *little* rough.

Eleanor, Zack and their bums were shaken around like beans in a can, bouncing and crashing off the walls, roof and floor.

It was almost a relief when they hit the emergency exit and it popped open, sending them flying out on to the ground in front of the Great White Bum and right into the middle of the Mutant Spew Lord puddle.

Almost.

CHAPTER 75

PUDDLE

'Get out of me!' said the Mutant Spew Lord puddle.

Zack, Eleanor and their bums were only too happy to comply with the puddle's request.

'Gross!' said Eleanor, jumping up and wiping the slimy goop off her clothes.

'Double-gross!' said Zack, shaking his arms and hands clear of the stinking muck. Being giant-brown-blobbified had been bad, but this was much, much worse.

Eleanor shook her head. 'You should have left him in that web, Zack,' she said. 'You should have let the bumantula take care of him. We would all have been better off . . . including the Mutant Spew Lord puddle.'

'Yes,' said Zack. 'I know that *now* . . . but I didn't know it then. If only I could go back and change things, I would, but I suppose it's not that easy, is it?'

'No,' said Eleanor. '*Nothing* is easy.'

But, as disgusting as they were, the remains of the

Mutant Spew Lord were the least of their worries at that moment.

The Great White Bum was purple with rage.

They looked up at his huge dark cheeks. 'You two!' he roared.

'Four, actually,' said Zack's bum, pulling Eleanor's bum out of the puddle.

'Whatever!' said the Great White Bum, shaking. 'I should have known that you would have one last desperately futile attempt to stop me from fulfilling my dream, but I never suspected that you would stoop as low as this. All is fair in love and war, but to break my heart in this way is unspeakably cruel.'

'Well, you'd know all about unspeakable cruelty,' said Eleanor. 'You killed my mother.'

'And mine,' said Eleanor's bum.

'And mine,' said Zack.

'And mine,' said Zack's bum.

'You've been responsible,' said Eleanor, 'for the deaths of *everyone* we loved, and you have the nerve to accuse *us* of unspeakable cruelty?'

The Great White Bum chuckled. 'Flattery will get you nowhere,' he said. 'But never forget, it was you and your kind who made me what I am!'

'By what twisted logic do you come to that conclusion?' said Eleanor.

'It was a long time ago,' said the Great White Bum. 'Back when I was just a hatchling. I was barely out of my shell when our nest was attacked by bum-fighters. They wiped out my whole family. They tried to kill me, too, but I outflew them. I took refuge on Uranus, where I was treated as a god by the local bums. I stayed for millions of years. I eventually returned to the Earth to rejoin my race, but discovered that all of my kind were dead, wiped out by an arseteroid. I realised I was the last of the Great White Bums. I thought I was destined to spend the rest of my life alone. That is, until I discovered the time-travel possibilities of the brown hole.'

Zack gulped.

Eleanor glared at Zack.

'Can you imagine what sort of welcome to the world it is to be shot at by bum-fighters?' continued the Great White Bum. 'If I am violent and vengeful, it is all *their* fault. *They* made me what I am!'

'Nobody *made* you anything,' said Eleanor. 'You made yourself.'

'Maybe,' said the Great White Bum. 'And maybe not. What is certain is that I am now making the way clear for the first, last and greatest life form on the planet!'

'With my help, of course,' said the Mutant Spew Lord puddle.

'*Your* help?' said the Great White Bum. 'A puddle of vomit?'

'Not just a puddle of vomit, Your Whiteness!' said the Mutant Spew Lord puddle. 'Your faithful servant.'

'Faithful servant?' said the Great White Bum. 'I've never seen you before.'

'Sir,' said the Mutant Spew Lord puddle. 'For many long years I was known as the Kisser . . . working for the B-team . . . but I was a bum-fighter in name only – a double-agent – working at every opportunity to sabotage their plans in order to help you establish the new world order. Let me continue to serve you. Let me be your right-hand man! Please . . .'

The Great White Bum regarded the puddle on the ground sceptically. 'You don't even *have* a right hand – *or* a left. And you don't even resemble a man. You look like you've been eaten by maggots, sicked up by flies and put yourself together again!'

'I have,' said the Mutant Spew Lord puddle, bubbling sadly.

CHAPTER 76

MOPPED UP

The Mutant Spew Lord puddle's reply took the Great White Bum so much by surprise that he began to laugh. The Prince took his cue and began to laugh as well. Maurice and the other Great White Bums joined in and the entire gathering began emitting great gales of methane-fuelled mirth.

Zack blocked his nose and looked at the puddle. Its bubbling had been replaced by steaming.

'What I want to know,' said the Mutant Spew Lord puddle as the laughter subsided, 'is, what's your excuse?'

'I beg your pardon?' said the Great White Bum. 'Excuse for what?'

'Your excuse for being a big pimply loser with half of his left cheek missing who doesn't know who his true friends are!' said the Mutant Spew Lord puddle.

Zack caught his breath sharply. It was not a good idea to talk like this to the Great White Bum. Even if it *was* true.

'Seize that puddle!' said the Great White Bum. 'And throw it into the Crack of Doom!'

'But how do we seize a puddle?' said the Prince.

'Mop it up!' said the Great White Bum, exasperated. 'Use the robot's dress!'

'No!' whimpered Robobum, who was lying on the ground. 'Not my dress!'

But the Prince and Maurice were unmoved by Robobum's pleas. They tore at her dress and began using large handfuls of it to soak up the puddle.

'You're making a big mistake!' said what was left of the Mutant Spew Lord.

'I don't make mistakes,' said the Great White Bum.

'Yes you do,' said the Mutant Spew Lord puddle. 'You fell in love with a robot, you big fat fool.'

The Great White Bum roared with fury. He grabbed the soggy pieces of wedding dress, containing the Mutant Spew Lord puddle, from the startled Prince and Maurice – and threw them into the fiery crevice himself.

A huge balloon of flame and steam erupted from the Crack.

And then silence.

CHAPTER 77

SQUASH!

The bum-fighters stared dumbly at each other. Nobody spoke.

They didn't have to.

They all knew what was coming next.

'Prepare to be squashed,' said the Great White Bum, surprising no one. '*Very slowly.*'

'You'll never get away with this!' said Zack.

'Oh really?' said the Great White Bum. 'And how do you propose to stop me? You are surrounded by thousands of Great White Bums – obedient to my every command – your devious time-travelling bum-mobile is broken and you are covered in a substance that even I must admit is rather unpleasant, and that's saying something.'

'I don't know,' said Zack, who knew the Great White Bum had a point, 'but we'll think of something.'

'Well, you'd better think fast,' said the Great White Bum as he began lowering himself.

Zack and Eleanor looked at each other.

Zack's bum and Eleanor's bum looked at each other.

Zack and Eleanor looked at their bums.

Their bums looked at Zack and Eleanor.

There was nowhere to run.

Nowhere to hide.

Nothing to say.

This was it.

They had lost.

All the pain.

All the suffering.

All the bravery.

All the stench.

All for nothing.

The whole glorious history of bum-fighting had come to a dead end.

Humanity was doomed.

The future belonged to the bums.

Eleanor picked up her bum and kissed it goodbye.

Zack hugged his bum tight, closed his eyes and prepared to be squashed.

Slowly.

CHAPTER 78

LOVE

'No!' cried a metallic voice.

Zack opened his eyes.

It was Robobum.

Somehow she had pulled her battered shell and body parts together for one last stand. 'Don't do it,' she said. 'They're not worth it!'

'Thanks a lot!' said Zack.

'I'm sorry,' said Robobum. 'But I must follow my heart!'

'But you're a robot,' said the Great White Bum.

'Robots have feelings too,' said Robobum. 'And my feelings are clear. I love you!'

The Great White Bum flushed pink as it absorbed what Robobum had said.

Then it flushed red.

Then it flushed a deep shade of crimson.

Its knees buckled.

Its flesh quivered.

'Are you all right, Your Whiteness?' asked the Prince.

'No,' said the Great White Bum. 'I am not all right. In my life I have experienced much – I have been kicked, smacked, pinched, forked, flicked, shot at, burned, feared, loathed and universally hated – but I have never experienced this. I have never experienced *love*.'

Robobum held out her arms.

Zack watched the Great White Bum visibly soften as millions of years of toughness and stinkiness and hatred melted away. He took a few faltering steps towards Robobum, but old habits clearly died hard. 'I am coming,' he said to Robobum, 'but first let me sit on them! Make them pay for how I've suffered.'

'No,' said Robobum. 'Just hold me.'

'First I'll squash them, and then I'll hold you,' said the Great White Bum.

'No,' said Robobum. 'I've got a better idea. How about first you hold me and then we'll squash them together!'

'You traitor!' said Eleanor. 'I'm glad Ned Smelly's not alive to see this.'

'Great bums think alike!' exclaimed the Great White Bum, stepping into Robobum's embrace. 'I can see we're going to have a long and happy life together!'

'Happy?' said Robobum. 'What is "happy"?'

'This, you big dummy!' said the Great White Bum, reaching out to Robobum.

'Oh, darling,' said Robobum as the two gigantic bums embraced over the top of the disbelieving – and completely grossed-out – bum-fighters.

'Yuck!' said Zack's bum.

222

'Now I've seen *everything*,' said Eleanor.

But Eleanor had spoken too soon.

Suddenly there was a loud crackling and hissing, and black smoke began to pour from Robobum's crumpled shell.

'What's the matter?' said the Great White Bum. 'What's happening to you?'

'Circuit overload . . .' spluttered Robobum. 'My system was not designed for "happy" . . .'

'NO!' cried the Great White Bum. 'I lost you once! I couldn't stand to lose you again!'

But there was no response from Robobum.

She was completely fused, her arms still locked around the Great White Bum.

CHAPTER 79

BOOM!

As the Great White Bum struggled to escape Robobum's embrace, there was a new commotion among the Great White Bums.

They were all pointing to the enormous blazing ball of doom hurtling towards them.

'Master!' cried the Prince. 'We must leave! The arseteroid is about to strike! We cannot delay any longer!'

'I can't move!' said the Great White Bum. 'Robobum has me locked in an unbreakable hug!'

'It's too late for you, now!' said Zack, with renewed hope. 'Too late for you and your demented dream of world bumination!'

But the Great White Bum's only response was to laugh. 'You stupid little boy,' he chuckled. 'You don't get it, do you?'

'I get it all right,' said Zack. 'You – the most evil bum in history – are about to be destroyed . . . *once and for all.*'

'That's where you're wrong,' said the Great White

Bum. 'I may be destroyed, but I won't be *destroyed*.'

'Huh?' said Zack.

'Let me put it another way,' said the Great White Bum. 'You can destroy me, but you can't destroy *me*.'

'Ignore him, Zack,' said Eleanor. 'He's got methane madness.'

'You wish,' said the Great White Bum, 'but I can assure you that I'm perfectly sane – although I think it's only fair to warn you, I'm going to be a little angry when I return from Uranus and find out what's happened.'

'You're not *on* Uranus,' said Eleanor.

'Oh yes I am,' said the Great White Bum.

'You're on Earth!' said Zack.

'That is true,' said the Great White Bum, 'but I'm *also* on Uranus. Remember?'

'Oh no . . .' said Zack, as the awful truth began to dawn on him. The reason the Great White Bum hadn't been killed in the original arseteroid collision was because he had been on Uranus at the time. He had only returned to Earth *after* the arseteroid had hit. But the arseteroid hadn't hit yet. And so the younger version of the Great White Bum that Zack had disturbed and chased 585 million years ago was *still* on Uranus. The Great White Bum was right. They could destroy him now, but it wouldn't mean they had destroyed him forever. The younger Great White Bum would return from Uranus. Bumageddon would still happen – and have to be stopped all over again.

Eleanor groaned. Zack turned to look at her. She had her head in her hands. It was obvious she'd realised the same thing.

'We've failed,' said Eleanor. 'Despite everything we've done, we haven't really changed anything.'

'No,' said Zack sadly. 'There are two Great White Bums. And we can only destroy one.'

'I suppose I should be thanking you,' roared the Great White Bum triumphantly. 'After all, with enemies like you, who needs friends?'

'You do!' said Zack's bum.

'Forget it,' said Zack. 'It's over.'

'It's over all right,' said Zack's bum. 'Over for the Great White Bum. Me and Robobum already took care of it.'

'Took care of what?' said Zack.

'The Great White Bum on Uranus,' said Zack's bum. 'While you and Eleanor were rescuing Eleanor's bum, and before the Mutant Spew Lord went crazy, Robobum and I were discussing the problem—'

'You *knew* about the other Great White Bum?' said Zack. 'Why didn't you say anything?'

'You were busy,' said Zack's bum. 'And it was very complicated. Anyway, to cut a long story short, we thought it best if I aimed Robobum's interplanetary death ray at Uranus and gave it a quick zap. Just to be on the safe side. If Robobum's calculations are correct, the death ray should be arriving on Uranus right about now, eradicating any form of life – including Great White Bums – on the planet.'

The Great White Bum gave a long loud moan of pain.

Zack and Eleanor stared dumbfounded at Zack's bum.

'I didn't know Robobum had an interplanetary death ray,' said Zack.

'There's a lot you don't know,' said Zack's bum. 'But it doesn't matter. You've got me.'

'I may not know much,' said Zack, shaking his head in wonder at his resourceful bum, 'but I do know one thing. You're the best bum a boy could ever wish for.'

Zack's bum reddened at the compliment.

Eleanor's bum looked on admiringly.

'Well done, soldier,' said Eleanor quietly. 'Well done.'

The Great White Bum moaned again – longer and even more loudly than before. The game was up. And he knew it.

'Eat arseteroid, you freak!' shouted Eleanor.

'You'll be eating it with me!' said the Great White Bum. 'At least I have that small consolation. You can no more escape than I can!'

'It doesn't matter to us,' said Zack, now finally understanding what his gran had meant, back in the stinkant cave. 'Where would we escape to anyway? This is where we *need* to be. Right here. Right now. This is what our whole lives have been leading up to. Because of us, the human race will be free to evolve without you constantly inciting our bums to rebellion. Because of us, bums will be free to work *with* their bodies instead of against them. There'll be no need for them to grow independent arms and legs and run around pursuing their own selfish interests . . .'

'I don't know if I like the sound of that,' said Zack's bum.

227

'It doesn't matter what you like or dislike,' said Zack. 'That's the whole point! Human beings will be completely integrated. No part will be more important than any other. All parts will work together in perfect harmony.'

'I *definitely* don't like it,' said Zack's bum.

'Me neither,' said Eleanor's bum.

'Don't worry about it,' said Eleanor, shielding her eyes against the heat and brightness of the arseteroid, which was now only minutes away from impact. 'You won't be around not to like it anyway. None of us will!'

'So long,' said Eleanor's bum. 'It was good knowing you.'

'You too,' said Eleanor, hugging her bum tight. 'And you, Zack,' she added, touching his arm. 'And your stupid bum. I'm going to miss you both.'

'I'll miss you both, too,' said Zack's bum, his voice cracking with emotion.

'Goodbye, Eleanor,' said Zack. 'And thanks. Thanks for everything.'

'And?' said Zack's bum.

'And what?' said Zack.

'Is there somebody else you want to thank?' said his bum.

'Ummm,' said Zack, '. . . oh yes! Of course.' He turned to Eleanor's bum. 'Thank you!'

'Don't mention it,' said Eleanor's bum.

'I hate you, Zack,' said Zack's bum.

'Oh well,' said Zack, reaching out and embracing his bum. 'Can't win them all, I suppose.'

His bum softened instantly and hugged him back.

The heat and light from the arseteroid were intense.

Suddenly Zack and his bum were drenched by an evil-smelling liquid.

'Errggghh, gross!' said Zack, wiping his face with his sleeve. 'What's that?'

'I don't know,' said his bum, looking up, 'but I think it's a tear. The Great White Bum is crying!'

Zack, Eleanor and Eleanor's bum looked up as well to see the Great White Bum as they'd never seen him before.

Not 'great' at all.

Instead they saw a sad, defeated bum standing at a crooked angle with sagging cheeks. Locked in the deadly embrace of a broken robot. Weeping.

'All I have worked for,' he sobbed. 'All I have lived for. All I have dreamed of. All for nothing. I've lost everything, including the only bum that I've ever loved. All gone. All past. All finished.'

'See you in Bumhalla!' shouted Zack as the fatal arseteroid completed the last few metres of its history-making voyage and slammed into the Earth.

CHAPTER 80

BUMHALLA?

Z ack blinked.

And blinked again.

But he couldn't see anything.

He wondered if he was dead.

Then he heard a screech.

Oh no, he thought.

It's not over.

What was it now?

A deadly tyrannosore-arse on the prowl?

A tricerabutt getting ready to charge?

A pouncing poopasaur?

A bumodactyl swooping in to carry him away to its nest in the mountains?

But more important than 'what' was 'why'.

Why was he hearing anything at all?

He was supposed to be dead.

He'd just been hit by an arseteroid the size of a major city with three thousand trillion megatons of destructive force. Enough force to completely wipe out 95 per cent of life and utterly change the course of history on Earth forever. Zack was a tough bum-fighter – that was for sure – but no bum-fighter was tough enough to survive an impact like that.

So, he figured, he *must* be dead.

And if he was dead, was he in Bumhalla?

Zack heard the tyrannosore-arse screech again and frowned.

If this *was* Bumhalla, then what was a tyrannosore-arse doing here?

He blinked again and, discovering with relief that he was now able to see, looked around him.

It sure didn't *look* like Bumhalla.

Bumhalla was supposed to be a glorious place where great bum-fighting warriors gathered to celebrate their heroic bum-fighting days.

But what Zack saw was just a cobweb-covered corrugated-iron roof, only a few metres away from his face.

It wasn't exactly what he'd expected Bumhalla to look like.

Somehow he'd expected the decor to be a little more upmarket.

A little more befitting honoured bum-fighters.

Pressed-gold ceilings, for instance.

Not cobwebs.

A large black spider crawled lazily across the roof towards a small fly struggling on its web.

Zack shivered as he watched the fly. He knew all too well how that felt. He reached up and pulled the fly free of the web.

Sitting up, he realised he was a long way off the ground.

He was sitting on top of an enormous stack of hay bales.

There was a gap, and on the other side of the gap there was another large stack of hay bales.

Smoke was wafting into the building from somewhere outside.

Old rusty bits of machinery and contraptions were hanging from the walls.

He heard the screech again.

But now it sounded less like a tyrannosore-arse and much more like a rooster.

Zack blinked again.

Nope.

He wasn't in Bumhalla.

That much he was sure of.

And he wasn't on prehistoric Earth.

As far as he could tell, the only immediate danger he faced was falling off the hay bale and being attacked by a rooster.

But what about Eleanor?

Where was she?

CHAPTER 81

BARNHALLA

'Eleanor?' called Zack.
   There was no response.
'Eleanor?' he called even louder.
'Zack?' said a voice from the top of the other hay-bale stack. 'Where are we? Are we dead?'
'I'm not too sure,' said Zack. 'But I don't think so. We seem to be in a barn.'
Zack watched as Eleanor sat up and rubbed her eyes. She coughed.
'How did we get here?' she said, peering over the edge of the stack and towards the open door, where there seemed to be some sort of bonfire burning. 'And where are our bums?'
'I don't know,' said Zack. 'Apparently this is what happens when you're hit by a gigantic arseteroid from outer space. You wake up in a barn with no bum.'
'I would have preferred Bumhalla,' said Eleanor.
'Me too,' said Zack. 'But who's complaining? At least we're alive.'

'Or we're dreaming,' said Eleanor.

'Even if we're dreaming, we're still alive!' said Zack.

'Not necessarily,' said Eleanor. 'We could be dead and just dreaming that we're dreaming that we're still alive.'

'But that's stupid,' said Zack, raising his voice. 'If we were dead, how could we . . .'

'You'll be dead if you don't get out of my barn right now!' yelled a figure standing in the doorway. 'How many times do I have to tell you kids that it's not safe to play up there? Your mothers will kill me if they find out!'

Zack and Eleanor both stared at the figure in the doorway. It was bright and their eyes were having trouble adjusting to the light, but as they did they saw, to their surprise, that it was Ned Smelly.

'Ned?' said Zack, wondering why he was dressed in a pair of farmer's overalls instead of his traditional bum-fighting armour.

'Ned?!' said Ned, walking over to the middle of the bales as Eleanor and Zack climbed down. 'Who's Ned?'

Zack looked at Ned and grinned.

'Why, you, of course!' he said. 'You're Ned. Ned Smelly!'

'Right, that does it!' said Ned, his face turning crimson with anger. 'I've had enough of you two! Get out of here and don't even think about coming back again until you've learned some respect!'

Zack and Eleanor stood there, too surprised by Ned's outburst to move.

'Well?' he said. 'What are you waiting for? Get out!'

He waved his pitchfork and moved towards them threateningly, but Zack and Eleanor didn't need any more encouragement to leave.

They ran.

CHAPTER 82

ED

Zack and Eleanor ran out of the barn, past a smoking bonfire and down a long dirt driveway.

They didn't stop running until they came to a gate. They clambered over it and stood on the other side, trying to catch their breath.

'What was all that about?' said Eleanor. 'Why do you think Ned was upset?'

Zack was holding on to a letterbox as he panted, and noticed a small painted sign hanging from the bottom.

'I don't know,' said Zack. 'But I think it might have something to do with the fact that his name is not Ned Smelly.'

'Huh?' said Eleanor, standing up with her hands on her hips, looking back up the driveway in case Ned Smelly was coming after them. 'Of course that was Ned. Wasn't it?'

'Not according to this sign here,' said Zack.

Eleanor bent down and studied it carefully. 'Ed . . .

Kelly . . .' she said, reading aloud. 'Ed Kelly?'

'Ed Kelly,' said Zack, nodding.

After she had stared at it for a long while, Eleanor rose up slowly. 'Zack,' she said. 'Something's happened. Something big.'

'I know,' said Zack, nodding. 'But *what* exactly . . . and why are you staring at my bum?'

'Because it's where it's *supposed* to be, Zack,' said Eleanor, patting her rear. 'And so is mine!'

Zack reached around and patted his bum. Of all the strange things that had happened in the last few minutes, this was the strangest of all. His bum had been running around by itself for so long that he could hardly remember when it was last attached.

'Are you OK?' he said.

But there was no reply.

'Hey!' said Zack. 'Say something!'

He knew it was a dangerous command to give to his bum, but it remained silent.

'You're right,' said Zack to Eleanor. 'Something's horribly wrong. I'm worried.'

'I didn't say something's horribly wrong,' said Eleanor. 'In fact, I think it might be the other way around. I think that – for a change – something might have gone horribly *right*.'

'Eleanor,' said Zack, 'you must still be suffering methane madness – or at least you've inhaled too much of that bonfire smoke! Ned Smelly thinks he's somebody called *Ed Kelly*? And my bum isn't running around being a smart-arse? How can you call that "horribly right"?'

'Because *it's exactly what we wanted*, you idiot!' said Eleanor.

'But I thought "Ned Smelly" was a good name,' said Zack.

'Not that,' said Eleanor, 'though that's part of it. No, what I mean is that we've succeeded in creating a future where bums are *just* bums. The Great White Bum has been destroyed and the world has evolved exactly as it would have if he hadn't been encouraging bums to rebel against their owners for so many thousands of years!'

CHAPTER 83

BUM-FREE!

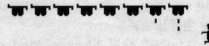

Zack thought carefully.

Perhaps Eleanor was right.

If she was, it would certainly help to make sense of the Blind Bum-feeler's predictions: 'Zack Freeman . . . hero of free men everywhere . . . past, present *and future* . . .' Here they were in the future, and men were now, apparently, free. But it still didn't make sense, thought Zack.

'You're forgetting one thing, Eleanor,' said Zack, frowning. 'We were directly underneath that arseteroid. Whether or not we succeeded, we shouldn't *be* in the future. We shouldn't be anything apart from a couple of fossils at the centre of the Earth.'

'You're wrong, Zack,' said Eleanor. 'We weren't *directly* underneath the arseteroid. Don't you remember? We were underneath the Great White Bum and Robobum.'

'You think we were protected from the force of that arseteroid by a couple of bums?' said Zack.

'Not just ANY couple of bums,' said Eleanor. 'The combination of the Great White Bum's blubber and the fully riveted reinforced steel cheeks of Robobum may have been enough to shield us from the worst of it.'

'But even if that's true, how did we end up here?' said Zack. 'Why aren't we just sitting around on the smoking shell of a dying Earth? Could we really be that lucky?'

'Maybe,' said Eleanor. 'And then again, maybe not. Brown holes are the result of an extraordinary amount of force. It's possible that at the moment of the arseteroid's impact, the force was *so* great that a temporary brown hole was created. A hole through time and space lasting only a mere instant – but long enough to suck us back to the future and spit us out in the present.'

'But,' said Zack, 'that means the Great White Bum might have survived the blast and been sucked back here as well!'

'No,' said Eleanor, shaking her head. 'Definitely not.'

'How can you be so sure?' said Zack.

'Because if he had been, our bums wouldn't be so much a part of us. They'd be running free. No, he – and Robobum – were destroyed in the blast. We were transported back. Evolution has been able to develop the rest of the world without the interference of the Great White Bum. Give or take a few minor details, of course.'

Zack pondered Eleanor's words.

'So we're the only survivors . . .' he said. 'Just us and Ned . . . I mean, *Ed* . . .'

'Maybe,' said Eleanor, her eyes widening. 'And maybe not. Did you hear what Ned – I mean *Ed* – said? He said, "Your mothers will kill me." *Mothers*, Zack. He said *mothers*!'

CHAPTER 84

HOMECOMING

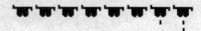

Zack could see exactly where Eleanor was leading. 'Come on, Zack,' she said excitedly. 'Let's go home!'

'Wait!' said Zack, grabbing her shoulders and making her face him.

'What?' said Eleanor, impatiently. 'Don't you see, Zack? In a Great White Bum-free world there was no Great White Bum to kill my mother . . . my mother is still *alive*! I've got to see her!'

'Be careful, Eleanor,' said Zack. 'If everything you've said is right, then, yes, she *could* be alive. But she might not be the same as you remember her.'

'I hardly remember her at all anyway,' said Eleanor. 'I was only four when she died.'

'I'm just saying, don't get your hopes up too high,' said Zack. 'That's all.'

Eleanor nodded. 'All right, Mr Gloomy,' she said. 'Can we go now?'

'Wait,' said Zack. 'One more thing. We'd better

not tell anybody about what we've been through. If you're right, and there's no such thing as runaway bums and bum-fighters in this world, then they'll think we've gone insane.'

But Eleanor was already running.

Zack took off after her.

CHAPTER 85

MARBLETON

Zack and Eleanor ran all the way from Ed Kelly's farm into Mabeltown. But as they passed the Mabeltown sign they were in for another surprise. It didn't say Mabeltown. It said: *Marbleton*.

Even so, the change didn't faze them too much. Not after their run-in with Ed Kelly. They were starting to get the hang of the new world. Everything was the same, just slightly different. Or was it that everything was different, but just slightly the same?

Neither Zack nor Eleanor particularly cared as they ran through the streets of Marbleton, which Zack was relieved to see was exactly the same as Mabeltown except that it bore no evidence of the devarsetating bum attacks that he had witnessed the last few times he was there.

There weren't even any skidmarks on the road, except for those left by cars.

'Not like that!' yelled a familiar voice, as they hurried

244

past the local football club. A large, brawny football coach, wearing a jumper with black-and-white stripes and cut-off sleeves, was showing a group of kids how to kick a football.

Zack smiled and pointed him out to Eleanor.

'Look,' he said. 'It's the Kicker!'

Eleanor nodded and smiled too, as the Kicker dropped the ball on to his boot and kicked it clear out of the pitch.

'*That's* how you kick a ball,' he yelled at the terrified children.

'Same old Kicker!' said Zack.

'Yeah,' said Eleanor. 'Some things never change.'

They turned the corner into the main street. As they passed the local bakery, they heard a series of sharp cracks. The sign on the window read *S. McKerr's Bakery*. They could see a large woman brutally kneading and smacking a lump of dough into submission.

'The Smacker!' said Zack. 'I've really missed that sound!'

Suddenly Eleanor clutched Zack's arm. 'Zack!' she said, pointing at a shop across the road. 'Look! Captain *Sterne*'s Fishing Supplies!'

Zack's eyes grew wide. The window was full of fishing rods, tackle boxes, nets, wellington boots, full-body wetsuits and a range of lethal-looking spear guns. One of the larger spear guns looked just like the bum-harpoon that Zack had used to shoot the Great White Bum.

'Do you think . . . ?' he said.

'Yes!' said Eleanor, walking even faster.

'Look over there!' said Zack, as they approached a small used-car lot that was surrounded by strings of coloured flags.

A well-dressed man with a moustache and slicked-back hair was standing outside watching them as they passed. Zack stared at him. It was the Kisser!

'Good afternoon,' he called. 'Either of you interested in a car? I have some great bargains . . . how about a fun-mobile?' he said, pointing to a little beach buggy.

'Cool,' said Zack. 'But I'm not old enough to drive.'

'Pity,' said the used-car salesman, looking at Zack with a twinkle in his eye. 'I think it would really suit you. Come back when you're old enough. I'll do you a very special deal. Trust me!'

'Thanks,' said Zack, winking at Eleanor. The Kisser certainly looked a lot better than when they'd last seen him, but he was still up to his old tricks.

'See?' said Eleanor, when they were well past. 'The details might be different but the people underneath are still the same.'

'Yes,' said Zack, with butterflies in his stomach.

They were approaching his grandmother's street.

'I hope you're right . . .' he said. 'I really do.'

CHAPTER 86

ALIVE!

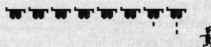

As they walked down his gran's street, Zack was startled by a cat jumping out from behind a tree. It rolled on its back in playful recognition of him.

'Mittens!' said Zack, overjoyed to see her alive again. He knelt down and patted her head. As he did so, he imagined that he felt his bum twitch. His bum and Mittens had never got on very well.

'It's not Mittens, Zack!' said his gran's voice. 'It's *Muffin*.'

Zack looked over the fence into his gran's front garden. There, bent over a bed of pink snapdragons, was his gran. She was pulling weeds out of the ground with the strong fingers that had made her so famous as the Pincher.

'Leave the boy alone, Mabel,' said an old man who was balanced on top of a small stepladder, washing a front window of the house. He was wiping the glass dry with a large handful of newspaper. 'Mittens, Muffin . . . what's the difference? It's all the same to a cat. How are you, Zack?'

Zack was too stunned to speak.

It was one thing to see your grandmother who died sixty-five million years ago alive again, but to discover that your long-dead grandfather who you'd never even met was still very much alive was another thing entirely. It was Percy. *Percy Freeman. The Wiper!*

'Hi, Grandpa,' said Zack, his voice sounding very far away to him, as if speaking in a dream. 'It's a great honour to meet you.' His grandpa gave Zack a strange look. 'I mean, *see* you,' said Zack, flustered as he realised his mistake. 'It's good to *see* you again!'

'It's good to see you again, too, Zack,' said his grandpa, chuckling. 'Even though you've only been gone since this morning.'

Zack looked at Eleanor and frowned. 'I have?' said Zack.

'Are you feeling all right, Zack?' said Gran.

'Yes,' said Zack quickly. 'I'm fine. Are . . . are . . . Mum and Dad home?'

'They're over at Eleanor's house,' said his gran.

Zack turned to Eleanor. 'They're alive!' he said.

'Of course they're alive, you silly boy!' said Gran, peering closely at Zack. 'I think you must have been out in the sun too long today.'

'No,' said Zack. 'I just forgot.'

Gran shook her head and laughed. 'You forgot your parents were alive?' she said. 'You'd forget your own head if it wasn't screwed on!'

'It's not Zack's head that's the problem,' said Eleanor. 'It's his bum.'

'Language, young lady!' said Gran.

'Sorry,' said Eleanor.

Grandpa winked at Zack and Eleanor, trying to suppress a grin.

Zack smiled. The details were different, but the important things hadn't changed. She was still the same old Gran.

'Anyway,' she said, 'you two had better be getting along to Eleanor's house. You're having dinner there tonight – or had you forgotten that as well? They'll be wondering where you are.'

Even as she spoke, Eleanor and Zack heard a voice calling to them from across the street. They looked and saw two men sitting on the decking at the front of the house.

'Eleanor! Zack!' boomed a deep voice. 'Dinner's almost ready!'

'That's my dad,' said Eleanor, her eyes shining.

'You'd better go,' said Zack's grandpa.

'See you later,' said Zack, as he ran to catch up with Eleanor, who was already halfway across the street. 'Have a good night.'

'You too,' called Gran. 'And don't forget to wash your hands!'

CHAPTER 87

STORIES

Zack stared as he approached the house. His father was sitting next to Silas Sterne.

'They *are* alive!' said Zack as he drew level with Eleanor.

'Yes,' said Eleanor. 'But what about our mothers? Where are they?'

'Probably inside,' said Zack.

'I hope you're right,' said Eleanor, biting her lip.

The two bum-fighters – or, to be more accurate, *ex*-bum-fighters – walked up the front steps. Smoke filled the air.

'. . . but you know, Jim,' said Eleanor's father, a red glow coming from the end of his pipe, 'I don't think I'll ever forget the sound that the Great White Whale made when I hit it with the harpoon. I think it will haunt me to the end of my days.'

'In a strange way, I know exactly what you mean, Captain,' said Jim Freeman. 'I've never been whale-hunting, of course, but once in the middle of a symphony my bassoon made a noise very similar to that of a whale in distress. An interesting sound, to be sure, but definitely not appropriate for that passage. The conductor never forgave me. I think that sound will haunt me to the end of my days as well.'

'So you really *do* play a wind instrument,' said Zack, shaking his head in wonder. 'In an orchestra!'

'Of course I do!' said Jim. 'You know that!'

'About time you two showed up,' said Captain Sterne, turning his attention to Eleanor. He opened his arms wide. 'You were supposed to be home an hour ago!'

'Sorry, Dad,' said Eleanor, embracing her father.

'You two haven't been playing in Ed Kelly's barn again, have you?' said Captain Sterne, pulling a bit of straw out of Eleanor's hair.

'No,' said Eleanor, straining to see into the kitchen through the door. 'Is Mum inside?'

'Yes,' said the Captain. 'She's with Judi.'

'I'll just go and tell her that we're OK,' Eleanor said, rushing inside.

The kitchen door banged shut behind her.

'Always on a mission, that girl,' said Captain Sterne.

'Just like her father,' chuckled Jim.

The Captain fixed Zack with a glittering eye as he packed a new pipe. 'I was just telling your dad about my time aboard a whaling ship.'

'You were a whale hunter?' said Zack.

'A whale *hunter*, yes,' said the Captain. 'I never actually caught one. I came close, of course, but the Great White is a slippery beast . . .'

Zack nodded distractedly. He was more interested in the sight of Eleanor hugging her mother. And the sight of his own mother standing next to them.

'Have you ever read *Moby Dick*, Zack?' said Silas.

'No,' said Zack, desperately trying to hear what Eleanor was saying to her mother above the Captain's ramblings.

'I had to rescue Zack from a drain . . . and then we got lost in the desert . . . Brown Forest . . . Sea of Bums . . . bumcano . . . zombie bums . . . maggots . . . brown hole . . . Uranus . . . dawn of life . . . bumosaurs . . . bumantula . . . bumodactyl nest . . . Stink Kong . . . Crack of Doom . . . Great White Bum . . .'

Zack heard Eleanor's mother laugh. 'What an imagination you have!' she said.

'We *didn't* imagine it!' said Eleanor. 'It really happened!'

Eleanor's mother, a kind woman with soft eyes, put her arm around Eleanor's shoulder and walked her to the door. 'You're not boring Zack with another one of your "true" stories, are you?' she said to her husband. 'It's easy to see where you get it from, Eleanor, with a father like that!'

'But, Mum!' said Eleanor. 'It's not a *story*! I'm telling the truth!'

Zack's mother looked at Zack. 'Eleanor's been telling us that you've had a very big adventure this afternoon,' she said, smiling.

'Tell them it's true, Zack,' pleaded Eleanor. 'They think I'm making it up!'

'Don't believe a word of it,' said Zack firmly, frowning at Eleanor. 'It was just a game.'

Eleanor glared back at him.

'I'm glad I can count on at least one of you to tell the truth!' said Eleanor's mother, shaking her head. 'Now, go and wash for dinner.'

CHAPTER 88

BEGINNINGS

I n the bathroom Zack and Eleanor washed their hands.

'We can't tell *anybody* about what happened and what we've been through,' said Zack, towelling his hands dry. 'They'll never understand. They *can't* understand.'

'I know,' said Eleanor. 'Sorry, I forgot. Seeing Mum again after all these years . . . I didn't know what I was saying. I still can't really believe it.'

'Yes,' said Zack, nodding. 'It's weird. It doesn't seem real. And yet it is. We did it, Eleanor. *We saved the world!*'

Eleanor turned the tap off. 'Do you think so?' she said. 'Really? You don't think there's even a slight chance that the Great White Bum survived? Remember what the Mutant Spew Lord said? *The Great White Bum is a freak.* How do we know that he didn't survive the blast . . . that he's not out there somewhere . . . plotting . . . planning . . . preparing another Bumageddon?'

254

Zack put his hands on Eleanor's shoulders. 'Because we're here now,' said Zack. 'That's how. You said it yourself!'

Eleanor nodded slowly. 'Yes,' she said. 'But—'

'No buts,' said Zack. 'Although it only feels like an hour ago to us, the arseteroid blast happened sixty-five million years ago. If the Great White Bum had survived, he would have tried something by now, don't you think? But there's no evidence of it. We're living in a world where there are no such things as bum-fighting or bum-fighters. Except for us, of course. We'll always be bum-fighters. And it is up to us to guard the Earth against the remote possibility of bum attacks in the future. We've both taken the bum-fighter's oath, after all. But we're the only ones who can ever possibly know what really happened and what we achieved.'

'Only us,' said Eleanor, 'and our bums.'

'No,' said Zack. 'Not even our bums, remember? They're not independent operators any more.'

As Zack said this, he patted his bum – and froze.

'What's the matter?' said Eleanor.

'It's gone!' said Zack. 'My bum's gone!'

Eleanor patted the back of her jeans and gasped. 'So has mine!' she said. 'Oh no! Not again! It's *not* over, is it?'

The two ex-bum-fighters stared at each other for a long, horrifying moment.

Then Zack grinned.

'Why are you smiling, Zack?' said Eleanor. 'This isn't funny!'

'Look!' said Zack, pointing over Eleanor's shoulder.

Eleanor turned. Then she grinned too.

Their two bums were standing on the window ledge, hand in hand, gazing at the sunset.

Eleanor and Zack stood and watched their bums watching the sunset.

It was a beautiful scene.

Well, beautiful until Zack's bum did a long, loud fart.

Eleanor's bum reddened, turned to Zack's bum and then, to both Zack and Eleanor's surprise, replied in kind.

The two bums nudged closer to each other as their gases mingled and combined into a perfect love heart above them.

Zack, his eyes watering, looked at Eleanor and smiled. 'No,' he said, 'I don't think it's over yet. Not by a long shot. In fact, I think it's only just begun.'

GLOSSARY

Accident
Another word for *fate*.

Anti-giant-brown-blob spray
Provides personal protection against *giant-brown-blobbification*.

Arseteroid
Irregularly shaped bum that orbits the Sun. They range in size from a 1,000-km diameter down to dust particles. Occasionally they slam into the Earth. Avoid. See *giant arseteroid*.

Atomic bum-blasting bullets
Bum-gun bullets with atomic bum-blasting power.

Atomic power punch
A powerful punch delivered to a bum, or bums. May be delivered with one fist or two. See *double-handed atomic power punch*.

AWOL
Arse without leave.

B-force
Unit of force based on the amount of energy it takes one bum to kick another bum one metre.

Blind Bum-feeler, The
A person with the power to 'read' bums and reveal amazing – but frequently mystifying – information about the past, present and future.

Blob-boy
Insulting term used to describe young *bum-fighters* who have been found fossilised inside fossilised *giant brown blobs*.

Book of Bumageddon, The
Ancient text that contains a prophecy of *Bumageddon*: 'And enormous bums will conquer the world and complete and utter devarsetation will follow. *Giant brown blobs* will rain down upon the Earth for forty days and forty nights. An evil stench will cover the land. And the reign of the *Great White Bums* will begin. Bums will rule the world again as they did in their glorious prehistoric past.'

BPS
Short for bum positioning system. A means of determining geographical location by means of one's bum.

Brown Forest, The
Formerly known as the Black Forest, this once healthy and thriving forest is now dead and brown and full of *stinkbogs* due to the presence of the Great Unwiped Bum, *Stenchgantor*. Avoid.

Brown holes
Very similar to black holes except brown. They are formed when vast interstellar bums run out of gas and collapse under the power of their own repulsive stench, which reverses itself and endows the newly formed brown holes with the power to suck anything and everything into themselves. Nobody knows what happens to matter sucked into a brown hole, but there is a strong possibility that the forces inside a brown hole are strong enough to form wormholes in the fabric of the *univarse* – wormholes powerful enough to allow vast interstellar distances to be travelled in the blink of an eye or even, perhaps, to permit time travel.

Brown Lake, A
Waste usually found at the bottom chamber of a *bumcano*. Avoid.

B-team, The
A crack bum-fighting unit made up of *the Kicker*, *the Kisser* and *the Smacker*.

Bum
The two fleshy mounds above the legs and below the hollow of the back. Detachable, with a will of their own. May emit gas. See *fart*.

Bumageddon
Destruction of the world by bums. Avoid. See *Book of Bumageddon, The*.

Bumageddonised
To be destroyed by *Bumageddon*.

Bumantula
A large prehistoric bum with hairy cheeks, big sharp fangs and eight legs. Likes to build webs across ravines and catch *bumodactyls* and unwary *bum-fighters*. Avoid.

Bum attack
Physical assault, either by ground, sea or air, by one – or more – bums. Avoid.

Bumbliteration
Result of particularly devarsetating *bum attack*. Avoid.

Bumcam
Tiny camera fitted on a bum. Can provide 180 degrees of vision. May be linked to other bumcams around the Earth via satellite to provide a comprehensive bum's-eye view of the world.

Bumcano
An extinct volcano colonised by bums and filled with lethal amounts of methane. Avoid.

Bum creeper
Rampant creeping plant notable for noxious-smelling flowers. Avoid.

Bum-fighter
Any individual engaged in bum-resistance, in either a paid or voluntary capacity.

Bum-fighters' Army pocket knife
A pocket knife with many additional items that fold into its handle, e.g. bum-screw, bum-file and bum-opener.

Bum-fighter's certificate
The minimum qualification required to become a professional *bum-fighter*. Involves a basic grounding in all aspects of attack, defence and hygiene.

Bum-fighting recruits
Promising young members of the *Junior Bum-fighters' League* who have been selected for a place at *Silas Sterne's Bum-fighting Academy*.

Bum-fighting simulator
Virtual-reality machine invented by *Silas Sterne* to simulate a wide range of bum-fighting environments and challenges, used for training new *bum-fighters*. The simulator is so powerful that the users forget they are in a simulated environment and actually believe that they are fighting bums.

Bum-gun
All-purpose anti-bum weapon. Fires a wide variety of ammunition, including drawing pins, staples and rusty nails.

Bumhalla
A glorious place in the sky where great *bum-fighters* and *bum hunters* go after they die.

Bum hunter
A bum-warrior who has given up regular bum-fighting in order to concentrate his or her energies on hunting big-game bums. This occupation is so fraught with danger that only a few of the bravest, most talented and smartest bum hunters survive.

Bum-mobile
Multi-purpose all-terrain bum-fighting vehicle. May have time-travel capability.

Bumnuts
The fruit of *bumnut trees*. These are similar to coconuts except the shells are soft and consist of two main chambers rather than one. Bumnuts are edible, but taste like burned toast.

Bumnut trees
Very similar to coconut trees, with a tuft of branches sticking out of a long slender trunk. *Bumnuts*, which look like bums, grow in small bunches on the branches.

Bumodactyl
Extinct flying bum of the Jurarssic and Cretaceous periods. Has membranous, leathery cheek-wings and a rudimentary but razor-sharp beak. Avoid.

Bumolution
Theory that bums were the first forms of life on Earth and that all subsequent life forms developed from them. See *Sir Roger Francis Rectum*.

Bumosaur
Extinct bums that ruled the Earth for hundreds of millions of years until the impact of a *giant arseteroid* rendered the Earth unsuitable for the continuation of the species. See *bumantula, bumodactyl, Great White Bumosaur, poopasaur, Stink Kong, tricerabutt, tyrannosore-arse*.

Bumquake
Just like an earthquake, only wobblier. And smellier. Avoid.

Bum-to-bum resuscitation
A method that bums use to revive each other.

Captain Sterne's Fishing Supplies
A comprehensive one-stop fishing supplies shop in *Marbleton*. Fresh bait every day.

Catastrophic time-travel error
Going back into the past and altering something that changes things in such a way that it decreases or eliminates the chance of you being born in the future. Or destroys the world. Avoid.

Crack of Doom, The
Formed by a dramatic fissure in the earth. Breeding ground of the *Great White Bumosaurs*.

Crapalanche
Just like an avalanche except crappier. And browner. And smellier. Avoid.

Destiny
Another word for *fate*.

Dirty double-crossing stinkant-bum-kissing loser with no friends
A very nasty thing to say to somebody . . . even if they *are* a dirty double-crossing stinkant-bum-kissing loser with no friends.

Double-handed atomic power punch
A powerful two-fisted punch delivered to a bum, or bums. See *atomic power punch*.

Double-handed cheek-lock
Particularly brutal and effective bum-wrestling hold.

Eleanor Sterne
Ferocious *bum-fighter*, dedicated to destroying the *Great White Bum* after it killed her mother in a surprise attack on a family picnic when Eleanor was only five. Daughter of legendary *bum hunter*, Silas Sterne.

E-mission
Task or project undertaken by a *bum-fighter*. Not to be confused with 'emission', which is something else entirely (see *fart*).

Ex-Mutant Spew Lord
Mutant Spew Lord that has been sucked into a *vacuum cleaner* and converted to a thin, watery puddle of blood and rotting flesh in the process.

False bum
Silicon-based imitation bum. May be *self-wiping*.

Fart
A small explosion between the legs. The exact size, duration and intensity of the explosion, however, will vary, depending on various factors, including age, weight and diet of the individual. Highly flammable. Avoid.

Fate
Another word for *accident*.

Final Pongflict, The
The ultimate showdown between bums and humans in the battle for *world bumination*. See *Bumageddon, pongflict*.

Flicker, The
Legendary *bum-fighter* highly skilled in the art of towel-to-bum combat. Member of the world's first bum-fighting team, *Mabel's Angels*.

Forker, The
Legendary *bum-fighter* highly skilled in the art of fork-to-bum combat. Member of the world's first bum-fighting team, *Mabel's Angels*.

Future present
The present moment that you will experience in a future moment. See *past future present, past present, present, present present*.

Giant arseteroid
Super-big *arseteroid* thought responsible for ending the reign of the *Great White Bumosaurs* 65 million years ago.

Giant brown blob
Gigantic, brown and blob-like. Avoid.

Giant-brown-blobbification
To be completely engulfed by a *giant brown blob*. To be avoided at all costs. See *Blob-boy*.

Giant mutant blowfly
Adult form of *giant mutant maggot*. Avoid.

Giant mutant maggot
Larval form of *giant mutant blowfly*. Avoid.

Giant mutant zombie blowfly
Adult form of *giant mutant zombie maggot*. Virtually indestructible. Avoid.

Giant mutant zombie maggot
Zombie-bummified giant mutant maggot. Avoid.

Great Unwiped Bum, The
See *Stenchgantor.*

Great White Bum, The
A rogue bum regarded by many as the most evil bum in the *univarse*. There are many theories about its origins. Some believe it to be a mutant bum created as a side effect of nuclear testing in the Pacific. Eric Von Dunnycan, in his book 'Chariots of the Bums', claimed that the Great White Bum was a space traveller who arrived on Earth thousands of years ago. Others believe the Great White Bum has been around for even longer and that it dates back 650 million years to the Pre-Cambrian period. Avoid.

Great White Bumosaur
The largest and most obnoxious of all the *bumosaurs*. Probably the first land-dwelling bums to emerge from *the Sea of Bums*. Avoid.

Great Windy Desert, The
A blisteringly hot, terrifying wilderness devoid of all life except for *needleweeds*, *stinkants* and *Ned Smelly*.

Henry
Zack Freeman's middle name.

Hokey-cokey
A really stupid dance, but quite good for amusing small children. Also good for sending *zombie bums* into a mysterious trance that enables you to pretty much lead them anywhere. Avoid unless you are a small child – or a parent desperately trying to amuse a small child – or your town is about to be overrun by zombie bums.

Holy buttrimony
A state of wedded bliss between two bums.

James and Judi Freeman
Zack Freeman's parents. Top-secret interplanetary *bum-fighters* who work undercover as musicians in the wind section of an orchestra.

Junior Bum-fighters' League
An organisation dedicated to the early identification of young people with bum-fighting potential. Offers bum-fighting clinics, training camps, a national bum-fighting competition and guest speakers. Contact the organisation in your nearest capital city.

Kicker, The
Legendary *bum-fighter* highly skilled in the art of foot-to-bum combat. Member of the famous *B-team*.

Kisser, The
Exceptionally charming *bum-fighter* highly skilled in the art of lip-to-bum combat. Less inclined to physical violence than the other members of *the B-team*, the Kisser was no less effective a bum-fighter, how-

ever, thanks to his formidable charm and lethal 'kiss of death'. Bumnapped and brainwashed by bums, he became a secret bum sympathiser and not only sabotaged the B-team's bum-fighting *E-missions*, but ultimately attempted to kill its members. See *Mutant Zombie Maggot Lord, The*.

Mabel Freeman
Zack Freeman's grandmother, Aka *the Pincher*.

Mabel's Angels
The world's first bum-fighting team, consisting of *the Flicker*, *the Forker* and, founding member, *Mabel Freeman*, *the Pincher*.

Mabeltown
Large country town named in honour of *Mabel Freeman* in recognition of her efforts as the founding member of *Mabel's Angels*, credited with inventing modern bum-fighting.

Maggotorium
Enormous underground chamber. The cold, dark and moist environment provides ideal conditions for maggots, Maggot Lords, *giant mutant maggots*, *Mutant Maggot Lords* and a range of other low-down scum-sucking parasites. Avoid.

Marbleton
Large country town named in honour of its annual marble-playing festival. The town is credited with the invention of modern marble-playing.

Maurice
Toadying servant of *the Prince*.

Methane madness
Delirium caused by exposure to high levels of methane. May cause hallucinations, visions, aggression, sudden mood swings, headaches and vomiting. Can be relieved with pure oxygen.

Mittens/Muffin
Mabel Freeman's cat.

Moby Dick
Fictional Great White Whale from the famous nineteenth-century novel of the same name by Herman Melville. See *Great White Bum, The*.

Mutant Zombie Maggot Lord, The
An exceptionally charming ex-human being (aka *the Kisser*) who, despite having his physical form mutated beyond recognition as a result of prolonged exposure to the extreme toxicity of a *brown lake* inside a *bumcano*, and then being eaten by *giant mutant zombie maggots* and regurgitated by *giant mutant zombie blowflies* and piecing himself together again, retains his persuasive powers.

Mutant Mutant Zombie Blowfly Spew Lord, The
See *Mutant Maggot Lord, The*.

Mutant Spew Lord, The
See *Mutant Maggot Lord, The*.

Mutant Spew Lord puddle
Remains of the *Mutant Spew Lord* after escaping from the *vacuum cleaner*.

Nailgun Series 9000
A popular *bum-gun* that fires high-velocity nails at its target (usually a bum). The 9000 series was notable for the innovation of using rusty nails capable of delivering a shot of tetanus as well as intense pain.

Ned Smelly
Bum-fighter who lives in the *Great Windy Desert*. Instrumental in helping to derail *the Great White Bum*'s plan to gas the world by means of a deadly *bumcano*. Brilliant inventor of *Robobum*.

Needleweeds
Weeds that look and feel like a cluster of sewing needles. The only plant tough enough to grow in the *Great Windy Desert*. May be eaten, but can cause excessive body odour, among other side efects.

Nuclear wart-head
Rough lump with explosive power.

Origins of the Univarse, The
Controversial bestseller by *Sir Roger Francis Rectum* in which he sets out his theory of *bumolution*.

Party pooper
1) Somebody who spoils the fun. 2) Popular party game for bums.

Past future present
A present moment that you experienced in the future but which is now in your past. NB: This is an extremely complex concept to get your head around and, to be honest, not really worth the trouble unless you're planning to do a lot of time travel in the near future. Or the near past. Or the distant future. Or the distant past, as the case may be. See *future present, past present, present, present present*.

Past present
A present moment that you experienced in the past. See *future present, past future present, present, present present*.

Perambulic merimbulator
The most important and complex component of a time machine, although they can be made from a tin and an old mattress spring if you are a brilliant inventor like *Ned Smelly*.

Percy Freeman
Zack Freeman's grandfather. Legendary *bum-fighter*, highly skilled in the art of toilet-paper-to-bum combat, aka *the Wiper*. Co-founder, along with *Mabel Freeman*, of modern bum-fighting. Unfortunately wiped out by *Stenchgantor, the Great Unwiped Bum*.

Pincher, The
Legendary *bum-fighter* highly skilled in the art of forefinger-and-thumb-to-bum combat. Founding member of the world's first bum-fighting team, *Mabel's Angels*.

Pongflict
Any conflict involving bums. See *Final Pongflict, The*.

Poopasaur
Big, lumbering and deadly. Lives in marsh and primeval *bumnut-tree* forests. Avoid.

Poopigator
Just like an alligator, except browner. And smellier. Avoid.

Prehistoric stinkant nest
Where *prehistoric stinkants* live. A typical colony can consist of up to 200,000 prehistoric stinkants and can have anywhere between 10,000 and 20,000 food and egg chambers. Avoid. See *stinkants*.

Prehistoric stinkants
Just like regular *stinkants* except much, much bigger. Avoid. See *prehistoric stinkant nest*.

Present
The present moment in which no past moments or future moments exist. See *future present, past future present, past present, present present*.

Present present
The present moment you are presently experiencing in the present moment. See *future present*, *past future present*, *past present*, *present*.

Prince, The
A bum with a very high opinion of itself. Toadying servant of *the Great White Bum*.

Robobum
State-of-the-art robotic bum designed to look like a *Great White Bum*. Fully riveted reinforced steel cheeks. Turbo-assisted jet-repulsion units. *Nuclear wart-head* equipped. Matter transport assisted entry and exit. Inside and outside voice options. Onboard tea- and coffee-making facilities. Also *self-wiping*. Invented by *Ned Smelly*.

Robospeak
To speak in a robotic manner.

Sea of Bums, The
A large inland sea teeming with aquatic bum-life. Many scientists believe that life on Earth originated in the Sea of Bums with single-cheek bum life forms.

Self-wiping
A highly desirable feature of both natural and artificial bums. See *false bum*.

Silas Sterne
Legendary *bum hunter* dedicated to hunting and killing *the Great White Bum*. Founder of *Silas Sterne's Bum-fighting Academy*.

Silas Sterne's Bum-fighting Academy
Founded by *Silas Sterne* in order to give new *bum-fighters* a solid grounding in the theory and practice of professional bum-fighting. It offers an initial three-month training course for a basic *bum-fighter's certificate*. Recruits can then go on to receive more advanced training and specialise in one or more particular bum-fighting techniques such as kicking, punching and smacking.

Simulated bum-fighting
See *Bum-fighting simulator*.

Sir Roger Francis Rectum
Author of *The Origins of the Univarse* – a controversial book in which Sir Roger set out his theory of *bumolution*. Also author of *What Bumosaur is That?*

Smacker, The
Legendary *bum-fighter* highly skilled in the art of hand-to-bum combat. Member of the famous *B-team*.

S. McKerr's Bakery
Marbleton bakery run by S. McKerr. Famous for her ultra-big ultra-soft buns.

Soap
A *bum-fighter*'s best friend. (NB: The first rule of bum-fighting is to always wash your hands afterwards.)

Stenchgantor
Also known as *the Great Unwiped Bum*, it is the ugliest, dirtiest, wartiest, pimpliest, grossest, greasiest, hairiest, stinkiest bum in the entire world. Or, at least it was, until *Zack Freeman* outstenched it with a pair of very smelly socks. The only bum known to have a nostril rather than an eye. Avoid.

Stinkant juice
Thick greasy liquid obtained from *stinkants*. Used for a variety of purposes, most commonly as fuel for robotic bums and *bum-mobiles*. One of the most powerful fuel sources in the world. Highly sought after.

Stinkant-napped
To be kidnapped by *prehistoric stinkants*.

Stinkants
Small red ants with a great big stink. The only creature tough enough to survive – and thrive – in the *Great Windy Desert*. Some varieties bite. May be eaten but can cause flatulence and serious body odour. See *prehistoric stinkant nest, prehistoric stinkants*.

Stinkbog
Area where a thick, sticky, stinky bog accumulates, trapping those animals, bums and *bum-fighters*

unlucky enough to fall into it and become preserved for future generations to laugh at. Avoid.

Stink Kong
Very large, very clumsy, very smelly, very stupid, very ugly *bumosaur*. Mortal enemy of the *Great White Bum*. Avoid.

Temporal navigator
Device used for navigating *bum-mobiles* through time.

Tricerabutt
Extraordinarily bad-tempered three-cheeked *bumosaur* with bony armour plating and a tusk-like wart growing out of each cheek. Avoid.

Twin-tyrannosore-arse attack
Attack by two *tyrannosore-arses* working as a team. Avoid.

Tyrannosore-arse
Large fierce flesh-eating *bumosaur* notable for the extreme redness and soreness of its enormous cheeks. Avoid.

Univarse
Everything that you can possibly think of plus everything that you can't. There are many theories about how the univarse began, but the truth is that most of the theories are just that. Theories. All that can be said for certain is that in the beginning there was a bum.

Uranus
Planet 2.871 billion kilometres from the Sun. It has seventeen known moons and eleven rings. Uranus's surface is an ocean of liquid methane which gives the planet a beautiful blue colour. NB: Extreme caution must be taken with the pronunciation of this planet's name to avoid potential confusion and embarrassment.

Vacuum cleaner
Electrical appliance that cleans surfaces by sucking dirt into a bag or plastic container. Also good for sucking up mutant puddles.

Wart-horns
Warts that have grown so big and hard that they've turned into tusks. Avoid. See *Tricerabutt*.

What Bumosaur is That?
Respected field guide to identifying and classifying all forms of *bumosaurs*. Written, illustrated and published by *Sir Roger Francis Rectum*.

Wiper, The
See *Percy Freeman*.

World bumination
Total domination of the world by bums.

Zack Freeman
A twelve-year-old boy who lived a perfectly ordinary life until two months after his twelfth birthday when

his bum ran away. To his utter surprise he discovered that he was an extraordinarily talented *bum-fighter*. He immediately put this talent to good use by saving the world from total *bumbliteration*. Twice. You can read all about his heroic deeds in 'The Day My Bum Went Psycho' and 'Zombie Bums from Uranus'. His grandmother, *Mabel Freeman*, was the inventor of modern bum-fighting. His parents, *James and Judi Freeman*, were secret bum-fighting agents. And *Zack Freeman's bum* was the next best thing to a lethal weapon. Together Zack and his bum formed a crack bum-fighting team and, with the help of *Eleanor Sterne*, a fierce bum-fighter in her own right, they were practically unbeatable.

Zack Freeman's bum
Bad, disobedient, argumentative, opinionated, cheeky, brave, resourceful, smart, cowardly, sensitive, kind, mean, romantic, stupid, and very very smelly.

Zack Freeman's parents
See *James and Judi Freeman*.

Zombie bum
A bum that is neither dead nor fully alive. Zombie bums feel no pain, have no thoughts or feelings and possess incredible powers of regeneration, which make them almost impossible to destroy. Driven to zombie-bummify potential victims, their only known weaknesses are extreme heat and a fondness for the *hokey-cokey*. Avoid.

Zombie-bummification
Parasitic attachment of a *zombie bum* to a victim's real (or artificial) bum. Turns the victim into an eating machine that exists for the sole purpose of making the zombie bum bigger and fatter than it already is. When the host is exhausted the zombie bum will simply abandon him or her and move on in search of a new victim.

Zombie-bummified
See *zombie-bummification*.

Zombie-bumvasion
Invasion of a place – or entire planet – by *zombie bums*.

Amuse your mates and embarrass unsuspecting passers-by with your

FREE FART RINGTONE!

To collect your free ringtone just fill in your details, including your mobile phone number, and send it to:

Bumageddon Ringtone Offer
Marketing Department
Macmillan Children's Books
20 New Wharf Road
London N1 9RR

My name: _____ My age: _____

My mobile phone number: _____

My parent/guardian's signature: _____
(You must get your parent/guardian's signature if you are under 12 years old)

Also from Andy Griffiths
(with quite good illustrations by Terry Denton)

Is this the right book for you?
Take the ANNOYING TEST and find out.

YES   NO

☐   ☐   Do you do ask, 'Are we there yet?' over
            and over on long car trips?

☐   ☐   Do you like to drive people mad by
            copying everything they say and do?

☐   ☐   Do you hog the shower and use up all
            the hot water?

☐   ☐   Do you enjoy asking silly questions that
            have no real answers?

☐   ☐   Do you swing on the clothesline when-
            ever you get the chance?

SCORE: One point for each 'yes' answer

3–5   You are obviously a very annoying
      person. You will love this book.

1–2   You are a fairly annoying person.
      You will love this book.

0   You don't realise how much fun being
      annoying can be. You will love this book.

Is this the right book for you?
Take the CRAZY TEST and find out.

YES NO

☐   ☐   Do you bounce so high on your bed
          that you hit your head on the ceiling?

☐   ☐   Do you ever look in the mirror and
          see a maniac staring back at you?

☐   ☐   Do you like to read stories about
          kittens, puppies and ponies getting
          mashed and pulverised?

☐   ☐   Do you sometimes get the urge to take
          your clothes off and cover yourself in
          mud?

☐   ☐   Do you often waste your time taking
          crazy tests like this one?

SCORE: One point for each 'yes' answer

3–5 You are obviously completely crazy.
     You will love this book.
1–2 You are not completely crazy, but you're not
     far off. You will love this book.
0   You are so crazy you don't even realise
     you're crazy. You will love this book.

Is this the right book for you?
Take the DISGUSTING TEST and find out.

YES NO

☐ ☐ Do you do any – or all – of the
following: pick your nose, talk in
burps or wee in swimming pools?

☐ ☐ Do you ever wear the same undies
two (or more) days in a row?

☐ ☐ Do you wish you knew the most
disgusting words in the world?

☐ ☐ Do you think Brussels sprouts are a
delicious mouth-watering treat?

☐ ☐ Do you like stories about dead flies,
giant slugs and mysterious brown
blobs?

SCORE: **One point for each 'yes' answer**

3–5   You are completelydisgusting.
        You will love this book.

1–2   You are fairly disgusting.
        You will love this book.

0   You are a disgusting liar.
        You will love this book.

Is this the right book for you?
Take the KIDDING TEST and find out.

YES NO

☐   ☐   Do you ever pretend that you are dead
           to get out of going to school?

☐   ☐   Do you like to ring up people you
           know and pretend to be someone else?

☐   ☐   Do you leave banana skins in the
           middle of busy footpaths?

☐   ☐   Do you own any of the following
           items: fake dog poo, rubber vomit,
           gorilla suit?

☐   ☐   Do you wish that every day could be
           April Fools' Day?

SCORE: One point for each 'yes' answer

3–5 You are a practical joking genius.
     You will love this book.
1–2 You are a good practical joker.
     You will love this book.
0   You are not a practical joker.
     You are what practical jokers call a 'victim'.
     You will love this book.

Is this the right book for you?
Take the STUPID TEST and find out.

YES	NO	
☐	☐	Do you worry about getting sucked into the top of esclators?
☐	☐	Do you push doors marked PULL and pull doors marked PUSH?
☐	☐	Do you believe a bogeyman hides under your bed?
☐	☐	Do you automatically turn round when somebody calls, 'Hey, Stupid!'?
☐	☐	Do you think that being able to stuff your mouth full of marshmallows is a sign of superior intelligence?

SCORE: One point for each 'yes' answer

3–5   You are extremely stupid.
       You will love this book.
1–2   You are fairly stupid.
       You will love this book.
0   You think you're really smart but deep down
       you're as stupid as the rest of us. You will love
       this book.

A selected list of titles available from Macmillan Children's Books

The prices shown below are correct at the time of going to press. However, Macmillan Publishers reserves the right to show new retail prices on covers, which may differ from those previously advertised.

All Pan Macmillan titles can be ordered from our website, www.panmacmillan.com, or from your local bookshop and are also available by post from:

Bookpost, PO Box 29, Douglas, Isle of Man IM99 1BQ
Credit cards accepted. For details:
Telephone: 01624 677237
Fax: 01624 670923
Email: bookshop@enterprise.net
www.bookpost.co.uk

Free postage and packing in the United Kingdom